The Mermen of Atlantis

The Mermen of Atlantis

Justin Mitson

Contents

One   One   **1**

Two   Two   **17**

Three   Three   **21**

Four   Four   **31**

Five   Five   **37**

Six   Six   **43**

Seven   Seven   **53**

Eight   Eight   **61**

Nine   Nine   **71**

Ten   Ten   **85**

Eleven   Eleven   **91**

Twelve   Twelve   **99**

Thirteen   Thirteen   **107**

Fourteen   Fourteen   **121**

Fifteen   Fifteen   **129**

About the Author   **135**

Red Team Ink
DBA of Zealot Solutions, Idaho LLC
9480 River Beach Lane
Garden City, ID 83714
Copyright © 2024 by Red Team Ink

All rights reserved. Without limiting the rights under the copyright reserved above, no part of this publication may be reproduced, stored in, or introduced into a retrieval system, or transmitted in any form or by any means (electronic, mechanical, photocopying, recording, or otherwise) without prior written permission.

This is a work of fiction. Names, characters, businesses, places, events, and incidents are either the products of the author's imagination or used in a fictitious manner. Any resemblance to actual persons, living or dead, or actual events is purely coincidental.

For permission requests or information about discounts for special bulk purchases please contact: redteamink@gmail.com. Substantial discounts on bulk orders are available to corporations, professional associations, and small businesses.

Printed in The United States of America
ISBN: 979-8-3304-9088-2
Title: The Mermen of Atlantis
Description: First Edition
Editing and cover design by Donna Lane

{ **one** }

Snowy peered at the spray rising from the ocean waves, just as she had a few days ago, and had an unsettling feeling, as if she was being watched. Nearby, the *Gillfish 2* crew loaded crates and other items to prep for their next voyage. She welcomed the sunny skies and gentle breeze. This trip to the Caribbean hadn't been as warm as she'd hoped, thanks to Kali's incantations and the creepy toad men. But since they'd been defeated, the weather had been much milder.

She turned to survey the buzzing crew and thought about returning to England, gray as it was. She missed her little cottage, with her observatory on the top, and Galileo stretched out on a sunny window seat. At least she knew Claudette and her daughters were taking care of the place. It would be good to be home again.

She jumped when a group of townspeople approached, lugging a wagon piled with stenciled white sacks tied with string. Its wheels skittered along the dock until it came to rest in front of Minty, who was talking with Mayor Jameson and Goldie.

"Miss Minty, we wanted to give you this flour," a woman said. "First Mate Carter said you enjoy baking. We'd like you to have it to show our appreciation."

Minty blushed. "Thank you," she said, hugging the woman. "That's very kind. And I've had a hankering to bake lately."

Snowy directed the crew to load the flour onto the ship then turned to Minty. "What are you going to make?"

"You know I always like to make cookies when I'm bored."

"I don't know that you'll be bored for long," Mayor Jameson interrupted.

"Why's that?" Snowy asked.

"These waters are frequented by pirates," he warned. "I'd be cautious about heading north-northwest. You won't run into them right away, but maybe in a day or two."

Goldie clutched Minty's green dress and hid her face in the fabric.

"I'm sure we can handle it," Minty announced, squeezing Goldie. "We've dealt with pirates before."

Snowy turned to the mayor. "Are there any reeds nearby?"

"Yes, in the marsh back there," he gestured. "Why do you ask?"

Snowy smiled confidently, "Could you have some of the townspeople gather up as many reeds as they can and bring them onboard while our crew finishes prepping the ship?"

"Of course," the mayor said. Soon there was a line of people depositing their bundles of reeds into an open barrel, at Snowy's instruction.

"Perfect," she said, as the last bundle was stuffed into the barrel. "Now we just need to lug this over to the engine room and fill it up with water."

"I'm on it," Clem said, and he whisked the barrel away.

Snowy inspected the dinghy they'd used to escape the warehouse. Clem and Rogers had loaded it onto the *G2*, and a few of the other crew members had already repaired it. Next, she turned her attention to the green silk balloon. It had torn in a few places, but she supposed Ari and Silky could mend it.

"I think we're about ready," Carter said. "What do you think?"

Snowy looked around. "I'd say you're right. And it's nice to be setting out in warm weather for a change. Captain Minty, if you please."

With that, Minty pulled on her tricorn and gave the command to shove off. They waved goodbye to the townspeople lining the dock and pulled away.

"It looks like there's a group of small islands northwest of here," Snowy said, looking at the map, another gift from the townspeople.

"And I'm hoping those will link up to the southern tip of the New World. It would be nice to see that on our way back to England—"

She abruptly turned and looked over her shoulder at the spray rising from the waves.

"What?" Minty asked.

Snowy blinked and looked harder. "Nothing, I guess," she said. "Just felt like we were being watched."

Minty raised a brow. "I think you might need a cookie. Or two. I'm going to make some."

"But who's going to—"

"First Mate Carter," Minty said, "will you take the helm, and let Goldie help?"

He squatted down to face Goldie, who was clapping with glee. "What do you say Goldie?"

"Yes!" she squealed as Minty took to the galley and started a batch of delicious spice cookies.

Snowy looked back at the sea again and shivered.

***

At dawn, Snowy woke to the sound of footsteps on the deck, several in quick succession. She dressed and went to investigate.

"Over there," said Rogers, pointing to a chain of islands in the distance as he peered through one of von Brock's spyglasses. "See it?"

Several crew members hurried across the deck, straining to look.

We've made good time, Snowy thought. But before she could congratulate the crew, she saw that it wasn't the island chain that had captured their attention.

It was a ship setting sail to the west, barely visible, with no discernable flags or markings. The sun had just begun its ascent on this peaceful morning, but Snowy had a sick feeling in her stomach.

"Sound the alarm!" called Carter, still pulling on his shirt after emerging from his quarters, with Minty right behind him. "Get everyone up and moving."

Soon, the deck was buzzing with the awakening crew.

"We'll skim by this island," Minty said, pointing to a small patch of land nearby. "That'll give us some cover. In the meantime, let's review the map in my quarters."

Minty, Snowy, Goldie, Carter, Clem, and Rogers went below deck and looked it over.

"These islands don't have names," Snowy said, leaning over the map, "but there are six clustered together. They're tiny, maybe just some shrubbery and a few trees, definitely not inhabited."

"But prime areas for pirates," Minty chimed in. "Do you think that's what we're looking at?"

Carter shrugged. "Can't say for sure, since that ship is unmarked, but this would be the perfect place for an ambush, if you ask me."

Snowy shivered again. They returned to the deck where she moved into action mode.

"Put up our colors," she ordered. "Let it be known that this is a British ship. And bring the boiler to full steam but be careful that it's not over stoked."

"Load those cannons and keep them at the ready," Minty yelled, picking up where Snowy left off. "I want that front cannon ready for a long-range shot."

Snowy peered through her best telescope, which Goldie had repurposed. "I'll get a visual on that ship," she announced. After a few moments, she said, "It seems to be plotting an intercept course. But we're moving too fast."

"They're raising all their sails," Carter broke in. "Trying to catch up."

"I bet we'll pass just out of range, in front of that ship," Minty called from the helm. "The best they can do is follow along behind or send up one lucky long-range shot. But I'm not worried."

"I am," Goldie cried. "I've never been in a pirate battle before."

"Bring up a dozen rifles, load them, and set them on the table at mid-deck," Carter instructed, and two crew members ran off.

Snowy peered through her spyglass again, noticing something. "Are those orange flags?" She lowered the spyglass. "We may be able to outmaneuver this ship using the islands and force them to turn."

"That would slow them down," Minty said.

"Exactly," Snowy agreed. "I just hope they're not—"

"PIRATES!" Rogers yelled, from behind one of Snowy's telescopes. "Looks like the Merciless Marauders of Madeira. Captain Sebastian Avery's crew. We're in trouble."

Snowy gasped. "Swashbuckling" Sebastian Avery led one of the most notorious, brutal pirate bands to sail the Atlantic. And unlike most pirates of the era, he had a full armada of ships, able to make quick work of any opponent. But he tended to roam the waters of the North Atlantic. Finding his crew this far south was an unexpected, and terrifying, surprise. Snowy caught her breath, thinking of all the horrible tales she'd heard about Avery, a coldblooded killer on a good day, and a remorseless, dastardly monster on his worst. His jewel-handled cutlass bore the gems of innumerable raids. And there was no telling how many throats he'd slashed with it, how many men had met their tragic fate at the tip of its razor-sharp blade.

"I'm scared!" cried Goldie, snapping Snowy back to reality.

"Bring up the dinghy," Snowy said, setting her jaw as the *G2* approached the island. "Disconnect the balloon but use the ropes to lower it over the portside. We'll need it on standby in case we need it."

"For what?" Minty asked.

"To escape, signal, connect with, or—"

"Capture those pirates!" Goldie exclaimed with a smile.

Clem soon had the dinghy prepped and ready. "We are ready, my captain," he said.

Minty gripped the brim of her tricorn, nodding at Clem and the others, who stood at attention. "Good work," she said. "Keep heading toward the island."

Snowy looked through her spyglass again, confirming what they all suspected. A black flag with a red-kerchiefed skull and crossbones was shinnying up the orange ship's mast, followed by a few others.

"They've hoisted the Jolly Roger," Snowy said, her eye tight to the spyglass. Then she noted the black and yellow four-square Lima, commanding the *G2* to stop, with a red flag directly beneath it. Snowy put the spyglass down, her heart sinking like an anchor at the grim sight. "And they've requested our surrender and will give us no quarter."

Minty looked at Snowy, who looked at Goldie, who then looked at Minty. They all exchanged a wink.

"Mr. Lancaster," Minty called to the sailor mounted at the top of the mast, "signal that we will accept this ship's surrender."

"*Their* surrender?" he uttered.

"You heard me," Minty said. "Get them to strike their colors. We are close enough to the island and at the ready. And they are out of range."

"Minty," Snowy said, nearly whispering, "has it occurred to you that there is a high probability that once we bank around this island, there will be more pirates waiting for us?"

"Perfect spot for an ambush," Minty whispered, recalling Carter's words. She took a deep breath. "Crew! As we turn, be on lookout for more ships."

The crew began murmuring, but Snowy put her hand up and they fell silent.

"Listen," she said, "the *G2* can outrun any ship, of that I'm certain. But we've never been tested by multiple ships, working together to plot and intercept. We could run straight into the jaws of the lion if we're not careful."

"But that ship will be swallowed by the jaws of the *Gillfish 2!*" Goldie piped up.

"That's the spirit," Snowy said as the ship began to turn toward the island's coast. "Minty, get ready to call out commands, and I'll let you know if there's anything we can do. We'll be ready to take the first shot with the forward cannon. If we adjust now, we could use it on the orange ship, but we'll lose our speed advantage. And Minty, I know you like to come in at full speed."

Minty nodded. "Goldie," she said, "I want you hunkered down in that little dinghy. It'll give you an extra layer of protection if shots ring out. But we may need you to help us, so keep your ears open and be ready for orders."

"Yes, Captain Minty!" she said, giving a snappy salute before darting off to the dinghy. The *G2* was nearing the coastline now, a few welcoming palm trees in sight.

"Steady as she goes, crew!" Minty called out.

"Stay cool under pressure," added Carter, swallowing a deep breath.

"Cool indeed," said Snowy, who then sprinted to her quarters, returning with the long wooden box that held the blue icicle. "Now," she said, catching her breath, "Carter, depending on what's on the other side of this island, can you pick your five best marksmen who are not already assigned to another task? We may need to set you up as a boarding party."

Carter started selecting his men and nodded to Clem that he might need to take over as first mate.

"I'll make you proud," Clem said.

Snowy pushed her glasses up her nose. She looked over at Minty. "We could use the dinghy to engage the pirates."

The crew placed six rifles in the dinghy, along with extra lead and powder. "Goldie," Snowy said, "on second thought, come with me. I'm giving you a very important job."

They went down to the engine room, and Snowy showed Goldie the boiler.

"I need you to drop a log in the burn box every minute or so," she explained. Then she told her which indicators to watch and how to turn the valve if the levels got too high. "This will give us the speed and maneuverability we need to turn and move without sails."

Goldie nodded.

"And now, for the most important part," Snowy said. "When I yell 'reeds,' you open that burn box and throw in as many reeds as you can, as fast as you can. Give them a shake to release most of the water, then throw them in. And then come back above deck. But only when I yell 'reeds,' got it?"

"Got it!"

Snowy went back to the deck and saw that they were nearly at the island's coast now. The crew was preparing the sails to turn along a rocky bend. But just as the *G2* began to rotate, the orange ship fired upon it.

"Ignore that ship!" Minty commanded. "They are out of range and just trying to distract us."

As she said this, the *G2* maneuvered around the outcropping, only to reveal a huge pirate ship sailing straight at them, with two more ships to its right flank, all bearing down at full speed.

"That's three ships," Carter called out.

Minty smirked. "Drop the main sail, launch the dinghy, and Snowy, fire when ready!"

Carter whipped his head around, about to say something. But before he could, Minty gave the wheel a heave and turned the *G2* so it was facing the largest pirate ship.

"Kotter cannon is ready!" called Snowy after checking the alignment.

"FIRE!" Minty ordered. An immediate report rang out, bewildering everyone at this close range. The cannon round flew straight into the center of the pirate ship's bow, cutting it into two pieces and sending an eruption of wood spiraling over the waves. Silence filled the air momentarily. Then Carter and his team launched the dinghy, quickly reaching the ship and boarding it.

"I didn't expect three more ships," Snowy said as she watched Carter and his team walk the pirate ship's crumbling deck. "Minty, I need to use some of your flour."

Minty was fiddling with the valves but nodded to Snowy. "Hard to starboard, port guns prepared to fire high. We don't want to hit Carter," she yelled down the gunner tube.

"Aye, Captain Minty," replied the sailor at the other end of the tube.

Minty looked over at Carter, who gave her a nod from the pirate ship's deck. With another spin of the wheel and turn of the steam valve, Minty turned the *G2* broadside, ready to take on the other two ships.

***

"We're cut off!" Lancaster yelled as the orange ship moved behind the *G2*, closing in.

But Minty wasn't about to panic. "Fire that port cannon!" she commanded. With a succession of short bursts, the *G2* struck one of the smaller approaching ships then blasted into the other. The cannon volley landed near the top of the second ship's mast, causing its sails to waver, but it wasn't enough to stop the ship from proceeding.

Minty turned and looked toward the orange ship. Carter was in front of it, situated in the dinghy and furiously rowing toward the *G2*.

"All four portside cannons now!" Minty cried. "Fire on the orange ship!"

In a flash, the cannons swung around and fired with devastating result, ripping it apart.

Turning back to the starboard side, Minty's eyes fixed on a second small boat, this one coming from the two smaller ships. Inside were four men, with a pair of rifles sticking out over the boat's hull. She gasped.

As it approached Carter's craft, one of the pirates yelled, "Let's take out that dinghy!"

But his threat was quickly met by a shot to the shoulder.

Minty lowered her rifle, still smoldering, and turned her attention back to the cannons.

Snowy was instructing the crew to load the bags of flour into all eight of the standard cannons.

"Maximum elevation!" Snowy called out. Then as they fixed the cannons, she yelled, "Reeds! Reeds! Reeds!"

"REEDS!" yelled Goldie from below, where she began piling the wet reeds into the fire box.

Minty almost choked as thick black smoke belched through the chimney at the *G2*'s stern.

"Flour power, fire!" Snowy yelled. And with that, all eight cannons shot a stream of white flour into the air, obscuring the *G2*. Minty hoped it would confuse the other ships and provide enough cover to keep everyone safe.

Meanwhile, in the water, Carter and Rogers had made their way between the two smaller incoming ships. Carter pulled on a glove and reached into his coat. With the white flour cloud as their disguise, he pulled out the blue icicle and thrust it into the warm Caribbean waters.

"Where did they go?" Minty heard one of the pirate crew call out. But before anyone could answer, the water around the ships froze solid. They lurched to a sudden stop, crashing into the ice. Carter's dinghy was thrust onto the ice's surface, sliding toward one of the ships, which was leaning on its side. In a continuous motion, he slipped the icicle back into its box, grabbed his rifle, hopped over the side of the dinghy, and charged toward the leaning ship.

While Minty watched Carter, she felt a tug on her dress. Goldie was coughing and gasping. She had left the boiler room as it filled with smoke. Minty put her hand on Goldie's back, patting it to comfort her.

"Where's Snowy?" Minty asked.

"She went down to help the cannon crew reload," Goldie said between wheezing coughs. "Why is it snowing?"

Minty scrunched her brows. "Snowing? OH! The flour—"

Just then Snowy came up to the main deck. Minty looked at Snowy, who looked at Goldie, who looked at Minty.

But Minty was worried. "I hope Carter's okay," she said, struggling to see through the black smoke and white flour cloud.

"Me too," Goldie said.

"He's smart," Snowy said. "I'm sure he's fine." She stopped and looked behind her, staring at the waves.

"What?" Minty asked.

Snowy shook her head as the spray from the waves rose in the air. "Nothing. By the way, do you know what we're rubbing against?"

Minty shrugged, completely unaware.

"On the portside," Snowy said. "We're still rotating but we're definitely in contact with something."

Minty realized Snowy was right. "Let's use our steam thrusters to move toward the orange ship and see if we can acquire it."

Goldie clenched Minty's dress again. But with the turn of a valve, the steam thrusters pushed the *G2* through the flour fog.

"Keep those cannons and rifles ready, men," Minty called out as she picked up her rifle again. "As soon as you see a clear shot, you take it." Then she joined Clem and other crew members while Snowy reloaded the Kotter cannon and Goldie climbed up the main mast, hoping to get a bird's eye view of what was happening. Minty watched as Goldie scrambled up the mast, then held her hand up to silence the crew.

"Do you hear that?" she asked over the hiss of the steam thrusters.

Snowy tilted her head. "Sounds like yelling."

Minty's eyes searched the area where she expected Carter to be, but the air was clogged with smoke and flour residue. She tried to focus in order to make out the words. But all she heard was splashes that seemed to be coming from near the ship, and the distant sound of arguing.

Fortunately, the thick air provided just enough cover for Carter's boarding party, which was silently climbing onto the deck of the listing pirate ship. As they crept along, the smoke and powdery clouds began to clear. Minty watched as Carter stopped suddenly, staring down the barrel of a rifle.

"Stay where you are," said a stodgy man, "or I'll blast your head clean off."

But just as the words left his mouth, the ship bashed against the ice again, sending the man with the rifle falling backwards. Rogers and the other men of the boarding party quickly tied up the pirate crew.

"Not so fast," called a voice from an elevated perch. Minty's eyes shifted and saw a man in a long, dark captain's coat, standing above Carter.

But again, the ship lurched, smacking into the ice. The captain bounced down the stairs, landing at Carter's feet.

"Get him and the officers in irons," Carter called out, and his men went to work. "Jones, stay behind and watch over them. Don't be afraid to use your rifle."

Jones nodded, and Carter and the others jumped down to the ice and ran toward the other ship, which was also beginning to sway against the frozen sea.

A light breeze had caused the smoke and flour clouds to dissipate by now. Goldie called down to Minty. "I see a dark shape," she said. "It's very close to us, but I can't tell what it is."

Minty gasped. "What does it look like?"

"I can only see a faint outline," Goldie said, squinting. Then she slid down the mast. "I think it's the orange ship. Look! They're right there!"

Minty swung her head around, auburn curls bouncing. The air was still thick on this side, but she could tell the ship was no more than thirty yards away. She called down to the gunner deck.

"Adjust those starboard guns down for close combat, and fire when ready," she instructed. "Hold the port cannons, just in case."

Within a moment's time, the broadside of the orange ship came into view, and the *G2's* cannons fired. But at such short range, the fire was withering.

"Rifle crew," Minty said, "fire!"

As the clap of rifles cut through the thick air, Minty saw a small white flag being waved from the orange ship.

"HOLD YOUR FIRE!" Minty ordered.

"We unconditionally surrender!" came the cry from the orange ship, as Minty watched it take on water and begin to list.

She returned her attention to Carter and the remaining men in the boarding party. They ran near one of the open cannon ports, sticking their rifles in and around the edges, and blasted directly into the ship's gunner deck. Minty could hear the commotion the shots had caused, and someone aboard the other ship was yelling, "We're on fire!" Soon, the pirate crew began spilling up to the top deck.

As they did, Carter reached to the end of his rifle and used the bayonet to dislodge the wedge break of the cannon wheel. Rogers and the other members of the boarding party helped give it a hearty push, and the cannon slid back, giving them ample room to climb in.

Minty held her breath as she watched some of the gunner crew turn back while some of the main deck crew began looking over the side of the ship.

Carter pulled the last of his men, Patterson, through the cannon port while Rogers ran headlong into the returning gunners. There was no time to reload their rifles, so they yelled like wild men and launched into hand-to-hand combat. Rogers was struggling, but as soon as Carter and the rest got there, they knocked the gunners cold and locked the bulkhead door.

"Let's move in closer," Minty called from the deck of the *G2*.

With the pirate ship's gunner deck secured, the rest of the crew banged on the door. Carter and the remaining four men surrounded one of the other cannons and turned it away from the open cannon port and toward the door. Then they lit the fuse and jumped over the other cannons in the row, hitting the floor with a succession of thuds. They covered their ears as the cannons went off. The gunner deck filled with smoke and everything went silent.

As the *G2* closed in on the pirate ship, Minty was fretting about what might be happening when she saw a man appear on an upper deck. He wore a very long coat and a tricorn.

Captain Sebastian Avery, she presumed, and a chill went up her spine.

"Who's down there?" he called to the main deck below.

After a few moments of silence, Minty heard a familiar voice.

"First Mate Noah Carter of the *G2*, and eight of my best men. We have your gunner deck. You have no choice but to surrender your ship or we will blow it up from below."

Eight? Minty thought. *Leave it to Carter to try to sound more intimidating.*

She exhaled as the *G2* made its approach, a slight smile turning her lips until she heard Avery again.

"You are mad! You can't win, Carter," he snarled. "Look at your pathetic crew, led by girls. You're no match for my men. Surrender now or my entire company will rush on my order and end you." Then he looked over at the *G2*, now sailing parallel. "And those girls."

Minty shivered, her rifle spent and the tumbling sea at her back as Avery advanced on Carter. Avery gripped the jewel-encrusted hilt of his cutlass and sneered. But his smug demand was met with the hollow click of Carter's flintlock, an additional weapon he'd tucked into his waistband in case he ran into a situation where the rifle wasn't practical.

"Tell that to the last lot who tried," Carter smirked, the pistol's cool steel fixed against Avery's temple. Resting his thumb on the frizzen, he narrowed his eyes. "We put Percival Savage in the clink at Maldon, and we'll gladly see you all hanged or coming up threes if you don't stand down. The choice is yours."

"Captain Savage?" Avery gasped. "You don't mean—"

"The very one," Carter said, leaning close enough to detect the catch in Avery's throat. Then he nodded toward the G2. "Thanks to those girls, he's rotting in a tower, tortured by the luring melody of crashing waves he'll never sail. With nothing but the tight, damp coat of his sins and four stone walls to keep him company for all eternity."

Avery gulped, droplets of sweat dampening his craggy brow as his knees began to wobble.

With that, Carter calmly cocked the hammer. "Now, would you care to join him, or are you going to be reasonable, Avery?"

As a random cloud of flour dust dropped in front of him, the pirate captain smirked. "I don't think you've got the guts."

Minty held her breath again, then noticed that one of the smaller cannons was rotating and now pointing straight up in the air. She peered through the flour cloud and saw it was Rogers turning the cannon.

"Oh, really?" Carter said, leaning into Avery's temple with his pistol. He drew the trigger back and Avery lunged forward with a jolt.

BOOM!

As Avery moved into the path of the cannon, Carter used his pistol to ignite the fuse.

KAPOW!

***

Avery's lifeless body fell to the deck, and his remaining crew members surrendered to Carter. Soon, they emerged from the flour cloud, and each of the ships raised white flags. Minty sailed the *G2* right up alongside the first pirate ship so she could hear what Carter and the captured pirates had to say. No longer obligated to express loyalty to their nefarious captain, they begged for mercy and made a staggering offer.

"Tell you what," said Bill Swift, Avery's first mate. "In exchange for our freedom, what if we turn over Avery's treasure?"

Minty's eyes widened. She couldn't even imagine the fortune Avery had amassed in his years pillaging the Atlantic. Not only was he one of the most ruthless scoundrels to sail the seas, he was also rumored to be one of the richest.

"Swifty," said Thomas Truehawk, "we swore to protect the captain's loot. We took an oath!"

Swift looked at Avery, sprawled in a splintered heap on the deck. Then he shot Truehawk a disdainful glance. "You want to end up like Avery, Tommy? There's no need to protect that murderous bastard or his assets anymore."

his waistband in case he ran into a situation where the rifle wasn't practical.

"Tell that to the last lot who tried," Carter smirked, the pistol's cool steel fixed against Avery's temple. Resting his thumb on the frizzen, he narrowed his eyes. "We put Percival Savage in the clink at Maldon, and we'll gladly see you all hanged or coming up threes if you don't stand down. The choice is yours."

"Captain Savage?" Avery gasped. "You don't mean—"

"The very one," Carter said, leaning close enough to detect the catch in Avery's throat. Then he nodded toward the G2. "Thanks to those girls, he's rotting in a tower, tortured by the luring melody of crashing waves he'll never sail. With nothing but the tight, damp coat of his sins and four stone walls to keep him company for all eternity."

Avery gulped, droplets of sweat dampening his craggy brow as his knees began to wobble.

With that, Carter calmly cocked the hammer. "Now, would you care to join him, or are you going to be reasonable, Avery?"

As a random cloud of flour dust dropped in front of him, the pirate captain smirked. "I don't think you've got the guts."

Minty held her breath again, then noticed that one of the smaller cannons was rotating and now pointing straight up in the air. She peered through the flour cloud and saw it was Rogers turning the cannon.

"Oh, really?" Carter said, leaning into Avery's temple with his pistol. He drew the trigger back and Avery lunged forward with a jolt.

BOOM!

As Avery moved into the path of the cannon, Carter used his pistol to ignite the fuse.

KAPOW!

***

Avery's lifeless body fell to the deck, and his remaining crew members surrendered to Carter. Soon, they emerged from the flour cloud, and each of the ships raised white flags. Minty sailed the *G2* right up alongside the first pirate ship so she could hear what Carter and the captured pirates had to say. No longer obligated to express loyalty to their nefarious captain, they begged for mercy and made a staggering offer.

"Tell you what," said Bill Swift, Avery's first mate. "In exchange for our freedom, what if we turn over Avery's treasure?"

Minty's eyes widened. She couldn't even imagine the fortune Avery had amassed in his years pillaging the Atlantic. Not only was he one of the most ruthless scoundrels to sail the seas, he was also rumored to be one of the richest.

"Swifty," said Thomas Truehawk, "we swore to protect the captain's loot. We took an oath!"

Swift looked at Avery, sprawled in a splintered heap on the deck. Then he shot Truehawk a disdainful glance. "You want to end up like Avery, Tommy? There's no need to protect that murderous bastard or his assets anymore."

{ two }

Nereus flicked his long, gleaming tail below the waves, steadying himself as he hid his pale green form against the rock. He couldn't believe what he'd just seen. Sebastian Avery's pirate ships had been terrifying his species for months. He and his merfolk had fled Atlantis, swimming to the south and west until reaching this spot near the island chains where the North Atlantic joins the Caribbean. Here, they had been safe from Avery's tall, imposing ships. But recently, they had lived in fear, as Avery and his crew seemed to have followed them to this location. Not only were these pirates ruthless in stealing treasure from every island they visited, they hunted Nereus and his merfolk for sport.

As the ruler of the merfolk, Nereus felt it was his duty to keep his species safe. There were whispers among his platoons that Nereus hadn't done enough to protect his mermen. They'd grown louder a few days ago, when he watched as one of Avery's men brought up a merman who had been entangled in a cargo net.

This young soldier named Kairus had barely learned to work his tail and glide through the seascape with his elder counterparts. Eager to please, he had volunteered to gather fish for the communal evening meal. But when he saw the large shadow cast down from the water's surface, his curiosity invited him to further explore. Though other mermen had warned him not to go past the borders of the reef, Kairus didn't listen. Soon, his tail was snagged in the net, and he wore himself out thrashing to get loose. When he was brought up to the ship's deck, Nereus and the others could only watch from their positions on the rocks.

Kairus dropped from the net with a harsh thud. Exhausted, he attempted to flop about. But the pirates surrounded him, poking him with long sticks as he gasped for air. His gills taxed and his body spent, Kairus was lifted by a trio of pirates, who then presented him to Captain Avery.

As they held him aloft, Kairus tried to speak. But Avery showed him no mercy. He plunged his jewel-encrusted cutlass into Kairus' abdomen and jerked it from side to side. A languid river of sparkling green blood, the color of Avery's looted emeralds, spilled onto the ship's deck. Avery's men cheered as the blood streamed forth. Then in his business-like manner, Avery beheaded him, holding up his trophy to even louder cheers. Grasping it by the blonde hair at the top of Kairus' head, Avery dropkicked it past the cannons, where some of his crew began kicking it around like a soccer ball. Then he slaughtered Kairus' remains into four equal parts. When he was finished, he called four of his officers over, then coldly instructed them to toss each quarter of Kairus' corpse from the bow, starboard, stern, and portside.

Horrified, Nereus watched as the left side of Kairus' torso bobbed along the waves and floated toward the rocks. A tiger shark surfaced, chomping into what was left of Kairus' body and dragging it below the water. Nereus was filled with feelings of guilt. Kairus had come to him personally, begging to enlist in Nereus' unit. Twice he had turned the lad down, saying he was too young. On the third attempt, Nereus finally relented, hoping he wouldn't regret his decision. Now it appeared that his worst fears had come true. And with Avery and his ships frequenting these waters, there was no telling how long Nereus and his merfolk could survive.

But now Avery was dead, his two most capable ships captured, and a third one destroyed. All at the hands of two young women with some very interesting technology on their unique ship. In a matter of days, it seemed that any threat Avery had posed had been eliminated.

A smile crept across Nereus' weathered green face, approaching the borders of his silvery-white hairline. As his long, wavy locks fluttered in the warm breeze, he felt the sunrays soak into the scales on his back. He inhaled deeply and took delight in presuming that this unexpected turn of events would help to re-establish confidence in his authority.

"Nereus," came a deep voice behind him.

He turned and saw Dorian, his first lieutenant, gliding toward the rocks where Nereus had taken cover.

"Sir," Dorian said, "what are you doing out here?"

Nereus glanced over his shoulder, his pale eyes, the color of flax, searching the waves. He turned back to Dorian, confident everything remained hidden.

"Just taking a moment to pay my respects to Kairus," he fabricated. "That poor boy didn't deserve such a fate, and I feel somewhat responsible for what happened to him."

At least that much was true.

Dorian nodded. "It is an unfortunate loss," he replied. "Are you going to address the colony? They're wondering what to make of that tense battle that occurred yesterday, and how it will affect our plans to remain here along the island chain. Some would like to return to Atlantis."

Nereus raised a silvery brow. "Do I detect a note of dissent among the ranks?"

"It's just that," Dorian began, "the reason we fled the North Atlantic in the first place was to get away from pirates like Avery. Now that he's dead, we think—that is, some think—that it would be safe to return to our way of life near Atlantis."

Nereus looked Dorian up and down. A burly merman with a long military career, Dorian had been a fierce rival as they both rose in the ranks. In fact, had Nereus not been able to best Dorian in combat, their situations might be reversed. Dorian was a dutiful subordinate, but Nereus always made sure to keep him on a short leash.

"Well," Nereus said, "I suppose it wouldn't hurt to gather everyone together and discuss our options. Why don't you swim back and tell everyone I'll make a speech, say in about two hours?"

Dorian saluted, raising a scaled hand to his blue brow. "Will do, sir."

Nereus returned the salute and nodded.

"Aren't you coming?" Dorian asked as he turned to swim back to the colony.

"In a little while," Nereus said. "I need a little more time out here."

With that, Dorian dove under the waves, his thick green tail disappearing in a neat column of spray. After a few minutes, confident that Dorian was gone, Nereus dove under the water. He started swimming in the other direction, near the location where Avery's third ship had sunk.

He passed squatty sailfish, jagged-mouthed barracudas, and a pod of spinner dolphins as he descended into the liquid blue curtain. Pushing himself along with his strong tail, he finally reached his destination, half-submerged on the sea floor. A small but thick oak chest, encircled with heavy chains, stuck out of the sand. Nereus ran his hands over the lock, already starting to rust.

"This will make a fine addition to my collection," Nereus surmised. "And with any luck at all, provide what I need when the time comes."

{ three }

Snowy looked over Avery's map, unable to decipher its markings. Besides, the land masses didn't look familiar. Wherever this treasure was located, she figured it'd be a while before they'd be able to look for it. Resigned to that fact, she carefully secured it in the *G2's* vault and went up to the deck.

It had been decided that Jones and Lancaster would pick two men each and oversee the return of the pirate ships to Bridgetown, with the *G2* following behind. The idea was to ensure that Avery's band of pirates would follow through on the conditions of their surrender. Then the *G2's* crew would reunite and finally head north-northwest, perhaps approaching the New World on the way back to England. It was a relatively easy sail with good wind and fair weather.

As Snowy came up to the deck, Minty was looking over the variety of instruments gathered from Avery's ships.

"Do you think any of this is useful?" Minty asked.

Snowy squinted in the setting sun and pushed her glasses up her nose. "Hard to say. I'd like to take a better look in the morning. I'm sure there are several things we can use."

"Shouldn't we at least offer them back to the pirates?" Minty inquired. "If they're going to restore their ships and use them to help protect the people here, they still need instruments, right?"

Snowy considered the thought while trying to examine a small spyglass in the dusky light. "I suppose," she said. She held the spyglass to her eye and looked through it. The view was hazy and undefined but she could swear she saw something. She turned it around, pulled her sleeve over the heel of her hand, and rubbed the objective lens. Then she looked through it again. It was distinct this time, a glimmering green tail, splashing against the waves as it disappeared into a column of spray. She pulled the spyglass away from her face, mouth agape, then looked again.

"This can't be!" she exclaimed.

Carter approached. "What can't be?"

Snowy searched the waves but saw nothing. "I think I'm losing my mind," she said.

"Do you need another cookie?" Minty chirped.

"What? No, I ..." Snowy began.

"I'll take a cookie," said Carter.

Snowy looked back at the water, empty. Then she looked at Carter. "Do you believe in mermaids?"

"Mermaids?" Minty chided.

But Carter nodded, calming Snowy's mind. "Actually, it's not uncommon in this area," he said. "I've never seen one, personally. But, there have been numerous reports of sightings throughout the Atlantic. This is my first time sailing this far south, but I've heard many other sailors say they've seen them. All the way from Gibraltar and working their way south, so I wouldn't rule it out."

Minty turned and looked at Carter, incredulous. "You don't really believe—"

But Snowy interrupted. "I would swear that's what I saw," she said. "A big, green tail disappearing into the water. Sort of iridescent, reflecting the sun's rays. And that feeling like I was being watched. Just now and the other day, too."

"That's ridiculous. Those are just stories sailors tell when they've been out at sea too long and they're bored," Minty continued, shaking her head in disagreement and crossing her arms. "Your mind is playing tricks on you. Right, Carter?"

"Ask some of those men," Carter said, motioning to the captured pirate ships sailing ahead of them. "They have more experience than I do. I bet at least a few of them will back it up. In fact, there are legends about all sorts of sea creatures in these parts."

Snowy cocked a brow at Carter. "Oh really? Like what?"

Minty uncrossed her arms and leaned closer.

Carter inhaled, "Well, let's see. There's the leviathan."

"That big sea serpent from the Bible?" Minty asked as the sun began dipping into the ocean.

"Yes," Carter said, removing his coat and placing it over Minty's shoulders. "Here, you're getting cold. Snowy, you too. Come share this."

Snowy stepped closer. "I've heard of the leviathan," she said as the warmth of Carter's coat stretched over her shoulder. "I don't think anyone really believes it, though."

"Well," Carter said, "just because you've never seen something doesn't mean it doesn't exist, right?" Carter asked.

The girls nodded.

"I suppose," Minty said. "But what other sea creatures do you think we might come across out here?"

Carter looked out at the horizon. Bridgetown was still several hours away. They'd likely not reach shore until morning. "Look," he said, "I know you girls are going to get to bed soon. I'll take over the helm tonight. I don't want to upset you before you try to get to sleep."

"What does that mean?" Snowy implored.

"Exactly," Minty piped up, "what are you not telling us?"

She focused her green eyes on Carter, and Snowy noticed that Carter seemed to look away.

"All right," he said. "But don't say I didn't warn you."

Snowy looked back at Minty. "Just tell us," she said.

"Well, there's a legend that these waters are home to the kraken," Carter said.

"The kraken?" Snowy scoffed. "Now I've heard everything."

"What's the kraken?" Minty asked.

Snowy pushed Carter's coat off her shoulder and wrapped it around Minty. "It's a mythical creature in Scandinavian folklore," she said. "A cephalopod."

"A cephalo-what now?" Minty said.

"Sort of like a giant octopus," Carter chimed in. "They can destroy a ship in no time."

"Yes, but I've only heard it rumored to dwell in the North Atlantic," Snowy said, peering into the dim water, her stomach beginning to clench. "These are tropical waters. We're way too far south for talk of any such thing."

"Just telling you what I've heard," Carter said.

"Well, I think it's all poppycock," Snowy said as she turned back to Carter and Minty.

"But you think you saw a mermaid," Minty pointed out.

Miffed, Snowy frowned. "You know what? I don't know what I saw." She peered over the ship's rail, perhaps trying to convince herself that there was nothing in that water except fish. "Minty," she announced, "I think Carter's right. I'm going to head down to my cabin and get to bed. Are you coming?"

Carter looked at Minty, exchanging a smile as she pulled his coat closer around her shoulders.

"Uh, I'll be down in a little while," she said.

"Suit yourself," Snowy said before retiring to her chamber.

When she got into bed, she tossed and turned. No matter how hard she tried to fall asleep, her head filled with gory images of terrifying sea monsters. In one of her visions, long, thick serpents with forked tongues wrapped themselves around the *G2's* steam thrusters, pulling it into the deep. In another, enormous tentacles lifted her off the deck and dragged her into the ocean as the crew helplessly stood by.

Snowy bolted upright in her bed, pulling the covers up to her neck. As her heavy breathing began to slow, she listened to the gentle crash of the waves against the *G2*, letting the soothing tones calm her.

"I've got to think about something else," she lectured herself as she settled under the covers again. She wondered briefly about the tails she thought she'd seen. Then, realizing she might start thinking about sea monsters again, her thoughts turned to Avery's map. She tried to recall the shapes and icons he'd used. They looked like nothing she'd ever seen before. But she could only imagine the treasure that map might lead to, and how much good she could do with it, investing in orphanages, housing, agriculture, and other programs to help people all over the world. It was with these happy thoughts that she finally surrendered to a peaceful sleep.

***

Minty stretched her arms above her head as she sat up in bed. The sun would be up soon. She had stayed up late, chatting with Carter on the deck as they sailed back to Bridgetown. After talking about everything from pirates and sea serpents to their shared experiences of losing their families and her favorite shortbread recipe, he finally made her get to bed sometime around eleven. The night had gone quickly, but she wanted to hurry up to the deck. By her estimate, they'd be approaching Bridgetown within an hour or two. And poor Carter surely needed some rest by now.

"Good morning," he greeted her as she strode onto the deck. "Did you get any sleep?"

Minty yawned. "A little."

He handed her a cup of coffee. "Here," he said. "I'm not going to drink it."

"Thank you. Besides, you should be getting to bed soon," she said, taking the cup.

He steadied the wheel and squinted, a thick mist filling the air. "No, I'm going to stay up at least until we reach Bridgetown," he replied. "I want to make sure Avery's men don't give us any trouble."

Minty nodded and sipped the coffee. "Speaking of Avery," she said as the warm liquid tickled her throat, "what did you think of his treasure?"

Carter looked back at her. "It's incredible," he said, eyes wide. "So many riches. Not just coins and bills but so much jewelry. And did you see some of the artifacts?"

Minty nodded, swallowing the last of the coffee. "I did," she said. "Some very unusual things in there. He must've really made the rounds, huh?"

"I'll say," he agreed.

A light breeze began parting the mist as the *G2* glided through the water, still following Avery's ships. Minty could see land on the horizon.

"Is that Bridgetown?" she asked.

Carter held a spyglass to his eye. "Looks like it," he said. "It'll be a while. We still need to sail around the coast, but I'd say we'll be back in Bridgetown in about an hour."

"That's great," said Snowy, who had just come up to the deck. "The sooner we turn these pirates and their ships over to Mayor Jameson, the sooner we can set sail."

"Back to Epping?" Minty asked, hope shining in her green eyes.

"Eventually," Snowy said, wiping the condensation off her glasses with her sleeve.

"Oh," Minty said quietly, unable to hide her disappointment. She had been hopeful they'd be able to take Goldie to England and get her settled soon.

"I was thinking we'd sail toward the New World," Snowy said as she put her glasses back on and adjusted them on her nose. "Doesn't that sound exciting?"

Minty managed a smile. "I guess."

Snowy turned to Carter. "What do you think?"

He caught Minty's eye and then looked at Snowy, shrugging his shoulders. "I mean, we've been at sea for a long time, but I suppose if we're already this close, it might be fun."

"That's the spirit," Snowy said, patting Carter on the arm. Minty narrowed her eyes.

"Oh, Snowy," she said, pulling Snowy toward her. "I've been meaning to ask. Do you think we'll need the balloon again? I mean, it seems like it could be useful."

Snowy wrinkled her nose as she thought about it. "I suppose it could be," she said.

"Maybe you should see if Ari and Silky can repair it."

"I'm sure they can," Snowy said.

"Great," Minty said, then nodded to Carter as she took the helm.

***

Soon, they reached Bridgetown, where Avery's pirates set foot on land for the first time in months. Carter, Clem, Rogers, and all the stronger men in the crew helped escort the pirates to the dock. Jones and Lancaster lugged a small chest behind the group and set it at Mayor Jameson's feet. Minty had grabbed Goldie and brought her to shore. Together, they watched as Snowy talked to Jameson, explaining that these men and their ships were to help defend Barbados as their sentence.

"I want you to be sure to treat them well," Snowy emphasized.

Mayor Jameson raised a brow.

"They may have done some bad things," she explained, "but they were willing to come here and serve their punishment by helping you and the people here."

Jameson smiled. "Well, sure. Everyone deserves a second chance to do the right thing. If they can stay out of trouble, we'll be happy to have reinforcements. Since we're a bit isolated, we can be quite vulnerable to the many threats these waters can carry."

"Threats?" Minty asked, stepping forward. "What kind of threats?"

"Well," Jameson said, "pirates, of course. But, well ... I don't know."

Minty turned to Snowy, who was already looking at her. She set Goldie down and motioned for her to go to Carter, who was sitting under a palm tree. He smiled when he saw the little girl run toward him, and patted the sand next to him, where she sat down and began drawing shapes.

"Are you saying there are threats besides pirates in these waters?" Minty asked.

"You know," Jameson said, dropping his shoulders. "People say things. Odd things. I don't really believe it. Sailors, you know. Tall tales."

"Like what?" Minty pressed. She didn't like the sound of this at all. First Snowy, then Carter, and now Jameson, all talking nonsense.

The mayor shook his head. "You know what? It doesn't matter. We sincerely appreciate you bringing us these men and the ships. I'll personally ensure that they're treated kindly."

Minty looked at Snowy, who, like her, didn't appear to be buying Jameson's dismissal of whatever threat he'd just implied. But she decided not to pursue it.

"Very well then," Minty said.

As Snowy went over the details of the pirates' release with the mayor, Minty walked over to join Carter and Goldie beneath the palm tree. She looked at the sand where Goldie had been doodling with a palm frond, making odd shapes.

"What are you drawing?" Minty asked.

"Something I saw in the water," Goldie replied.

"Is it a leaf?" she asked. "That's a big leaf."

Goldie shook her head. "No, guess again."

Minty looked at Carter, whose eyes were nearly closed. He looked peaceful in the shade of the palm. Minty felt bad that he'd been up for so long. She looked back at the sand.

"How about a claw? Like a giant crab?" Minty reached over and gently clamped her fingers down on Goldie's arm, mimicking a crab's claws.

"No!" Goldie squealed, rousing Carter from his near-sleep.

"Then I don't know what it is," Minty said. "Any guesses, First Mate Carter?"

He shook his head and yawned. "No, sorry."

Goldie giggled, "It's a—"

"Minty!" Snowy called, waving. "We're ready to sail. Let's go."

Carter stood and offered Minty his hand to help her up. As she brushed the sand from her skirt, Goldie exclaimed, "Race you to the ship!" and took off running. Minty looked back at the drawing, then shook her head.

***

Before long, they were back at sea. With everyone else at their stations or resting, Minty was daydreaming at the helm as they headed back toward the island chain. As the water splashed, she wondered what kind of treasure Avery had hidden. She gazed out at the waves, mostly calm as the *G2* chugged along. But on the horizon, something unusual caught her attention.

"That can't be," she said to herself. Then she picked up the spyglass and squinted. A shimmering green tail was slowly fading into a stream of spray ahead of the *G2*'s bow. She looked through the spyglass again, only catching the tip of the tail as it disappeared beneath the waves.

Minty started to call out, "Snow—"

But before she could finish, the *G2* was surrounded by bubbles and Minty felt her ship begin to sink.

{ four }

Nereus pulled the reins on his giant seahorse, commanding it to halt. He had been waiting for this ship to return ever since he saw it defeat Captain Avery's small fleet. Not only was this ship uniquely equipped with tools and artillery Nereus had never seen before, but the startlingly young crew—and two young women at that—were much more skilled than any group of sailors he'd ever encountered.

However, even with the Ahti gone, his species still faced great peril.

For months, the merfolk of Ahti, who generally kept to the north of these waters, had been threatening Nereus and his band, the Okeanos, which had swum south from Atlantis to live a life of freedom rather than succumb to a life of servitude to the Ahti. But, like Avery and his pirates, the Ahti had followed them. The Ahti had poached in the Okeanos hunting grounds, harassed their mermaids, and stolen some of their spears, crafted from whale bones. The Ahti outnumbered the Okeanos by at least two to one. Nereus knew he'd need to harness the power of this wondrous ship, and its crew, in order to defeat the Ahti once and for all.

He watched Endymion, a young ensign sent to the surface to cause a diversion, ripple through the water. He had done his job, luring the large ship back to this spot, where Nereus and his troops could now wrangle it under the depths. He pointed to Endymion, acknowledging his satisfaction, who returned the gesture as he took his place among the Okeanos soldiers in formation with Nereus.

"Get your lines in place," Nereus commanded from the saddle of his seahorse. And with that, his soldiers prepared their sinewy cords, fashioned from sturdy kelp stipes and the remnants of discarded fishing nets. At the ends were hooks made from sharpened coral fragments.

Another group, bobbing on giant squid, held onto wide-mouthed vessels as they waited behind the troops with the makeshift ropes.

He looked down the rows of his soldiers, neatly surrounding the outline of the ship that was slowly descending into the water. Dorian, Nereus' most trusted lieutenant, was positioned in front and gave a nod of confidence.

"Be ready to cast on my orders!" Nereus said. "And don't wait too long to get those oxidators in place on every one of those Landers. Time is of the essence with these creatures."

He had been eager for this opportunity, and for as long as he could remember, he'd had hundreds of his mermen lying in wait, ready to place these special air vessels over the heads of Landers. It was the best way he could think of to persuade them to help his cause.

Nereus looked at Fiz, a frail, ancient merman known as the master of bubbles, who resided at the depths of the Okeanos colony. Rarely leaving the ocean floor in his old age, he was a secret weapon who had developed the ability to isolate and manipulate various gases. With his long beard rippling under the water, Fiz nodded slowly to Nereus, indicating that everything was ready. As he did, Nereus noticed two teams of giant sea turtles, each team yoked to a large, double-handled amphora, their flippers waving in the water as they waited.

"Go!" Nereus called out and the sea turtles began to swim toward each other, lugging their massive Grecian pots. When they met, Fiz swam over and tapped each of the amphorae.

Immediately, a frothy spew of bubbles flurried from them, generated by the harnessed power of underwater volcanoes and pulsating toward the water's surface. Their rate and speed increased exponentially, creating a bubble fog that nearly enveloped the ship.

"Steady!" Nereus called out.

The bubbles continued to surge recklessly, creating such a force that all the mermen mounted on their seahorses began to sway in the resulting current. The mermen on the squid held tightly to their vessels to prevent them from floating away in the swelling stream.

"STEADY!" Nereus repeated.

While the Okeanos soldiers held their positions, the ship's hull descended, slowly at first and then, as the bubbles whirred, faster and faster.

"NOW!" Nereus screamed.

As the ship tumbled below the water, his mounted mermen cast their kelp and coral lines, securing their hooks into the ship's sides with precision.

"HOLD!" Nereus shouted, and every one of his troops held their lines until no slack remained.

The mermen on squid glided forward and everyone waited.

As expected, a young woman in a green dress, with long, auburn locks, began tumbling over the side of the ship. One of the mermen from the squid patrol swam upward, meeting her as she fell. Her arms and legs flailed as she tried to right herself under the water, but as she struggled, they slowed. Sinking now, her eyes began to close.

The merman calmly placed his glass vessel over her head, tucking her auburn tendrils inside. When he did so, her eyes opened, and she began to float effortlessly alongside him. Then he swooped her up and positioned her gently on the back of his squid.

A lean young man came next, falling from the ship, arms over his head as he dove toward the girl in the green dress. Before he could reach her, another merman on a squid intercepted him and placed an oxidator over his head. He resisted at first, but the merman put up his hands to show he meant the young man no harm.

Moments later, another young woman, this one with blonde hair and a blue and white dress, dropped from the ship. A young, blue-speckled lieutenant swam toward her. As with the other girl, this one struggled at first, but soon grew tired. As he put the oxidator over her pleasant face, she smiled and blinked her blue eyes. He clutched her in his arms as the sleeping gas inside the special breathing apparatus took effect. Nereus watched as she went limp.

As the remaining crewmembers came spilling out of the ship, the squid-riding mermen fitted each one with an oxidator over their heads, allowing them all to breathe underwater. A few of the squid patrol went through the ship's decks, making sure they'd retrieved everyone and gave them the life-saving glass breathing vessels. Then they gathered in a line and waited.

"Bring it down," Nereus instructed.

The mermen on their seahorses began tugging at the ship, pulling it toward a castle-like structure far below the surface. It had tall stone archways, festooned with algae clusters, and a lone tower. It took a while, but with all the mounted mermen working together, they managed to get the ship moving. Swimming in formation, the mermen dragged the ship to the structure, holding it steady.

"Get them all back on board," Nereus said, and the squid-riding mermen took their human captives onto the deck of the ship and waited again.

"Now, let's get that bubble over it," Nereus said.

By now, Fiz had hitched the sea turtle teams to a large gate. On his command, they tugged and the gate slid back from the floor of the structure. This released a giant bubble, which then surrounded the deck of the ship, extending about ten feet below.

"Perfect!" Nereus exclaimed. "Now, get these humans to the docking area. MOVE!"

He sat back on his seahorse and observed the Landers. The girl in the blue dress patted at her clothing, almost in a panic, until she pulled out a small box. She opened the lid and sighed in relief, then leaned against him, still woozy. Nereus wondered what might be inside the box. A secret treasure, perhaps?

"Lyr!" he called to his young lieutenant.

Lyr turned his head, revealing his blue-speckled face. "Sir?"

"You know what to do," Nereus said, shooting him a glance. "Make friends."

{ **five** }

Snowy let the air fill her lungs as she slid the matchbox closed, confident that Ari and Silky were safe inside.

"Is that better?" said a young merman.

She looked up at him and saw that he had kind eyes, soft like melting honey, that stood out in contrast to his glimmering, pale blue skin. Along his hairline, darker blue speckles disappeared into flowing golden locks that swept his shoulders. Suddenly, Snowy felt weak again, as if her legs might give out.

"What?" she asked, staring at him through her strange glass helmet. She'd never seen anything so intriguing.

"I asked if that was better, with the oxidator," he said.

She fiddled with the helmet's edge, resting gently on her shoulders. Though it wasn't uncomfortable, she was eager to remove it to get a better look at this wondrous creature.

"Don't do that," he cautioned, holding up his webbed hands. The pale blue webbing was nearly translucent and Snowy couldn't stop staring at it as he floated in front of her. "The oxidator is a special breathing apparatus. Every one of you Landers has been given one. It'll help you breathe down here. Keep it on, at least for now."

She nodded, looking around at the crew, seeing that they all wore these devices and that everyone seemed to be fine. Unsure of what to say, she stretched her hand toward the merman. But something solid yet transparent stopped her from making contact.

"What's this?" Snowy asked, her hand pressing against the barrier.

"It's an air bubble, protecting your ship," he explained.

Now Snowy ran both of her hands over the bubble's thin, smooth wall. It gave slightly when she pressed on it, but it didn't break. "Interesting. But protecting it from what?"

"Don't be afraid. I assure you that we mean you no harm," the merman said. "My name's Lyr."

"Lyr?" she repeated. "I'm Snowy."

"Pleased to meet you, Snowy. I've heard of snow. When we're in cooler waters, I've been told, we're swimming in the runoff from glaciers and ice floes." He smiled and looked her up and down. "I had no idea snow was such a lovely sight to behold."

Snowy felt her cheeks warm, a noticeable contrast to the cool ambient temperature inside her oxidator. Then she realized she had no idea how the *G2* and its crew had ended up so far below the sea.

"That's very kind of you to say," she said. "But I'm curious … if you mean us no harm, then why did you capture our ship?"

Lyr apologized, "Oh, I do hope you'll forgive us for that. You see, we are the Okeanos, who have traveled all the way from Atlantis to—"

"Atlantis!" Snowy exclaimed. "I thought that was just a myth."

"Well, Myth Snowy, I'm afraid you are myth-taken," he said with a wink.

Snowy surprised herself as she let out a hearty laugh, tickled by Lyr's play on words. A little levity in an otherwise uncertain situation was just what she needed.

Handsome and witty. Maybe this whole captured and dragged under the sea thing wasn't going to be so bad after all.

"That's clever," she said.

"I try," Lyr shrugged. "So, we swam south to get away from the Ahti, which is another band of merfolk. They have been preying on us, invading our hunting grounds, just being a general nuisance. And, we fear, they'll continue to escalate their attacks. Our leader, Nereus, saw your ship defeat a fleet of pirates and—"

"Oh yes, Captain Avery," Snowy said, recalling the battle and realizing her beautiful ship would now likely need repairs. "Wait, you said he *saw* us defeat the pirates?"

"Yes, that's what he told us," Lyr said.

"So then I *wasn't* crazy," Snowy said, remembering how she kept thinking she was seeing tails in the water and had the feeling that she was being watched.

Lyr scrunched up his speckled face, looking lost.

"That is," Snowy said, "I think I saw him, too. On the rocks not far from here. Well, not far from where we were when the ship ..." she trailed off as she felt something tickling her arm and floating along her waist. She worked her hands through a trail of seaweed vines and reached down for a small piece of pottery. "What is this?"

"The glass oxidators allow you to breathe, but they're fueled by your own personal air pot," Lyr explained. "Excess air bubbles out below the oxidator as you exhale. Then the seaweed holds everything together, so it can't become detached. Although, if you need to for any reason, you can pinch the seaweed and the device will release. But you'll always have breathable air as long as you have the oxidator."

"Fascinating," Snowy remarked, running her fingers over the seaweed strands and the five-inch air pot. It was thick in the middle, with curved handles at each side and wavy lines, which Snowy understood represented wind or air.

"You'll be able to take it off soon," Lyr said. "You just need to wear it for a while until you're acclimated. This way we can still talk to you, while you're inside the bubble and we're on the outside, here in the ocean."

"Unbelievable," Snowy said. "I've never heard of such a thing."

"Snowy," Lyr said, "do you remember falling overboard?"

Snowy put her hand up to scratch her head, then realized she couldn't.

"Let's see," she began. "I remember we were on our way back from Bridgetown, where we'd just dropped off Avery's men to help keep the peace and defend the island. I was down in my cabin, studying a map we'd just obtained from Avery's ship. Minty—that's my friend, our captain—she was at the helm and everything was fine. And then all the sudden, she called me, but before I could get there, I noticed there were bubbles forming all around the hull of the *Gillfish 2*—that's my ship, our ship. I thought maybe the steam engine was venting. I started checking the gauges and valves, but everything was normal. In fact, the steam engine wasn't even on yet, because we were in calm waters. And then ... gosh ... then there were so many bubbles all around the ship. Just everywhere. Millions of bubbles. And then they started popping—erupting, really—and before I knew it, the ship started to sink. See, with the buoyancy of the bubbles ... "

She glanced at Lyr, a look of consternation on his face indicating that he'd stopped following her somewhere around 'valves.'

I must sound like a crashing bore. How embarrassing.

"Well, anyway," Snowy continued, clearing her throat, "that's when the ship really started to sink. I was surprised because I thought the *Gillfish 2*, well, we call it the *G2*, was unsinkable. But down we went. I was desperate to grasp onto anything I could reach. It all happened so quickly. And I was so afraid for the crew. They're all such wonderful people. But I couldn't hold on."

Suddenly, she felt tense, agitated at the memory of what had just happened. It was all so chaotic, and she felt ashamed and helpless for not being able to take control.

"The last thing I remember was going over the rail. And then ... and then ..."

Lyr smiled gently, calming her. "And then you wound up here. But don't worry, Snowy. As I said, I assure you that we won't do you any harm."

"Then why are we here?" Snowy inquired.

Lyr placed his hand against the bubble, his webbed fingers pressing against hers. "Nereus said your ship has the equipment and artillery we need to defeat the Ahti."

Snowy flinched as her stomach tightened. "Our ship? I don't know that I want to—"

"Snowy," Lyr pleaded, "it's our only chance to defeat the Ahti. Nereus said you have some sort of cannon—"

"The Kotter cannon," Snowy said, squaring her shoulders. "It has specialized rifling that allows us to fire almost continuously. No other ship has one, at least not that I know of."

Lyr stepped back. "Sounds like it's not something to be *rifled* with," he said with another wink. "And neither are you."

Snowy couldn't help but burst out laughing.

I'll give him this. He's got a way with words and doesn't miss a beat.

"But how will our cannons be able to fire? Won't that, you know, burst the bubble?"

"Well," Lyr said, tilting his head. "I would hate to burst your bubble."

Snowy laughed again.

"But," Lyr continued, "we don't think they will. The bubble is tight enough that any projectile should leave a very temporary exit hole, allowing the bubble to seal up immediately."

"You think? You're not completely sure?"

Lyr shrugged. "Look," he said, "that's just what I've been told. Snowy, you seem like a good person. And awfully smart."

"Thank you," Snowy said, softening her shoulders.

"All I know is that the Ahti have made our lives miserable," Lyr went on. "And I don't think Nereus is going to take no for an answer. He's, well, he's not like you and me."

Snowy frowned. "I mean, I'd like to help—"

Lyr interrupted, "Snowy, I can't believe I didn't notice before."

"Notice what?"

"Has anyone ever told you that your eyes are the same color as the Eye of India?"

{ six }

Minty let out a sputtering cough and tried to focus. After a deep breath, she realized she was aboard the *G2*, but it seemed that the ship had been submerged. The horizon was blurry, and they appeared to be floating. Besides, there were all these ... mermen? Riding seahorses ... and ... squid?

She scanned the deck, and at the far end she saw Snowy, talking to a blue-speckled merman with golden hair that fell in waves at his shoulders. Minty shook her head.

How could this be?

She felt weak and nauseous, like everything was spinning. The last thing she remembered was sailing the *G2* away from Jamestown and seeing ...

She gasped.

The tail! I wasn't imagining it. Snowy and Carter—

"Minty, are you okay?"

She was comforted by the sound of Carter's voice behind her. She turned and instinctively threw herself against him. That's when she heard the loud clink of glass against glass.

"What's happening?" she asked frantically as he patted her gently on the back. "What's over our heads?"

"Shh, don't be upset," Carter soothed. "Everything's fine. They're called oxidators. The mermen put them on us. They're helping us breathe underwater."

"Underwater? Mermen? Noah, where are we? And Goldie! Where's Goldie?"

Carter pulled away, putting his hands on her shoulders. "Minty, calm down. It's okay. Goldie's fine. Don't worry. I just checked on her. She's looking at the seahorses, see?"

He pointed to the stern and Minty could see that Goldie, wearing her own little oxidator, was indeed looking at a group of seahorses, including a tiny little pink one that looked like it would be just her size.

"Whee! Giddy-up, sea pony!" Goldie called as she galloped in a circle on the deck while the seahorses floated just beyond her.

Minty turned back to Carter. "So, what happened? How did we end up down here?"

"Well," Carter said, "from what I can tell, they—these mer-men—pulled us down under the water. One of them told me when he put the oxidator on me. The *G2* is encased in an air bubble now, but we still have to wear these breathing devices, until we're adjusted."

Minty squinted her eyes and looked out toward the mermen, realizing that they were indeed floating just on the other side of a bubble.

"That is crazy," she said, blinking as if waking up from a dream. "This whole thing is crazy. I remember seeing a tail in the water. And just like Snowy, I thought I was seeing things. After that, I remember there were a lot of bubbles, and then we started sinking."

"Right," Carter said. "I was down in my cabin, asleep, and I felt the ship bouncing and jerking. While I was getting dressed, I heard you and Snowy yelling out orders. I hurried up to the deck as fast as I could and then I saw you go over the rail."

"I did? Oh, I did, didn't I? That's right. I went to see where the bubbles were coming from, but there were so many, and they were climbing up the sides of the ship, surrounding it."

"That's when I got to the deck," Carter said. "But then ..."

"They just swallowed me up," Minty recalled. "It was like the bubbles pulled me into them and the next thing I know I was under the water. I was trying to swim but the force from the bubbles was too strong."

"Lack of surface resistance," said Snowy, who had walked up to join them, an oxidator over her head.

"What does that mean?" Minty asked.

"The bubbles swallowed us up because there was no surface resistance, so the ship sunk," she explained. "Are either of you hurt? Minty, I saw you go over the rail, and then Carter ran past me and dove in after you."

Minty turned back and looked at Carter. "You dove in after me?"

Carter blushed. "I hope you're not mad."

Minty stepped back. "Mad? No, why would I—I mean, that was very brave of you, Noah."

"Well," he said, fidgeting with his hands and looking down at the deck, "I didn't want anything to happen to you. You're ... such a good captain."

"Thank you," Minty said, catching his eye as he looked up and offering a warm smile.

"So," Snowy said, "I need to talk to you about these mermen and the *G2*. See, I was talking to one of the lieutenants, Lyr. That's him over there."

She looked over her shoulder and waved at the blue-speckled merman Minty had seen her talking to earlier. Then she continued, "He says that Nereus, that's their leader, saw us fight off Avery's pirates and that he wants to commandeer the ship to help them battle this rival band of mermen, the Ahti. The Okeanos, that's what Lyr and the rest of them are called, they're especially interested in our Kotter cannon and they think it's their only chance to fight off the Ahti."

"Wait, wait," Minty said. "Commandeer our ship? Like we're their prisoners?"

Carter stood up straight, balling his fists.

"Well, not really," Snowy said. "I mean, kind of."

"Well, which is it?" Minty asked, growing impatient. "I'm not handing control of the *G2* over to anyone except someone on our own crew."

"Right," Carter chimed in.

"I don't really think we're being given a choice," Snowy said.

"And that doesn't concern you?" Minty snapped, a little surprised at the angry tone in her own voice. Even Carter jumped at her words. "What do we know about these mermen anyway?"

"Just what Lyr told me," Snowy said. "He said they don't mean us any harm."

Carter narrowed his eyes, looking at the mermen troops lined up on their seahorses at the far end of the deck. "And you believe that?"

Snowy hesitated.

"Do you?" Minty probed. "I don't know that I trust them, to be honest. They capture our ship and drag us down to the bottom of the sea, but say they don't mean any harm. Sounds kind of, you know, fishy?"

Snowy laughed. "Oh, that sounds like something Lyr would say," she said. "He has a funny way with words."

Minty crossed her arms, unamused. She knitted a brow and shot Snowy a glance. "Sorry, I don't buy it."

"Well," Snowy said, looking toward Lyr and smiling, "I think they showed good faith by putting those vessels over our heads so we could breathe. And this big bubble over the ship is keeping us all alive. If they meant to harm us, they wouldn't have done that."

Carter looked at Minty, who shrugged.

"I guess, but I still don't trust them," she said. "Maybe we're more useful to them alive than dead, for now. And then who knows what will happen."

She and Snowy stared at each other for a few moments. Minty fumed, trying to think of a good reason to trust these Okeanos, as Snowy had called them. They stood there, motionless, in uncomfortable silence.

"Oh," Snowy finally said, "Lyr's calling us over."

Minty turned and saw the blue-speckled merman swimming just past the bubble, holding a tall pitcher, and motioning for them to come closer. She looked at Carter, who nodded reassuringly, and they crossed the deck.

"Hello," Lyr said, holding up the pitcher. "You can remove your oxidators now."

Minty took hers off cautiously, then realized she was breathing just fine.

"I'm Lyr," he said. "You must be Minty."

"Yes," she said, still wary. "Hello. And this is No—err, Carter. First Mate Carter."

"Hello," Carter said after removing his oxidator.

"It's nice to meet you," Lyr replied, holding up the pitcher. "I thought you might appreciate some fresh water."

"Thank you," Snowy said, her voice almost bubbly. "You know what they say. Water, water everywhere, but not a drop to drink."

Minty turned and looked at her, thinking that was an odd way to talk to someone who was holding them captive.

Lyr pressed the pitcher against the transparent wall and into Snowy's awaiting hands. Instantly, the bubble resealed itself.

"That's amazing," Snowy said, taking a drink from the pitcher.

Even Minty had to admit it was amazing. "How did you—"

"Oh," Lyr said, "this bubble is made of whale mucus."

Snowy spit out the water and wiped her mouth with her sleeve.

"I know," Lyr said. "It sounds gross. But, it's very durable. Fiz, our bubble master, has worked for years to perfect this technology."

Snowy passed the vase to Carter, who offered it to Minty instead. She took a drink. Down here in the depths of the sea, it was good to taste fresh water again.

"This is very nice of you," she said to Lyr, softening just a bit. "How do you manage to have fresh water down here?"

"It's the Vase of Aquarius," Lyr explained. "It never has to be refilled. No matter what, it always pours fresh water."

Carter took a sip. "We have fresh water on the ship, thanks to our steam technology, but this is very refreshing. Thank you."

"It's the least we could do," Lyr said. "Now, if you'll excuse me, I need to attend to something. Snowy, I'll see you later."

"Bye," she said with a giggle, waving as he swam off.

Minty stared at her, confused by her behavior. Then she saw a mermen with pale green skin, much older than Lyr, approach them on a burly seahorse. The sight of him made her squirm.

"Ladies," Carter said, "don't look now, but I think that's Nereus coming toward us. Now, maybe it's not my place, to say this, but whether we trust them or not, it's probably a good idea to see what he wants and at least act like we're going to cooperate."

***

"Hello," Nereus said as he approached the trio huddled together at mid-deck. Dorian and Lyr flanked him. "My name is Nereus and I want to thank you for turning over your marvelous ship to us."

"But we haven't—" said the girl in the green dress, stepping forward.

Nereus glared at first, clenching his jaw until his gills puffed. Then he softened his expression into as warm a smile as his pale green skin would permit. "My child," he cooed, "what is your name?"

The girl matched his scowl, eyes focused on his less-than-persuasive smile. "My name is Minty," she said. "I'm the captain of this ship, and I'll decide—"

"Minty," he spoke over her, "you are being presented with a rare opportunity here, one you'd be wise to accept. How often are we afforded the chance to be on the right side of history?"

The girl's face remained rigid as she crossed her arms.

"Look," he said, "you have every right to be skeptical, but there's no need for that, child. We simply need to use your ship and its weapons. We mean you and your friends here no harm."

"So we've heard," said the other young lady, a bespectacled girl in blue.

"What Nereus means," Lyr interjected, "is that ... wait, none of us have been properly introduced."

With that, Lyr got everyone acquainted. Nereus observed the girls' postures begin to relax. In fact, the blonde one seemed much more friendly and willing to cooperate than the other. But he still couldn't read the young man between them, this First Mate Carter. Probably wise to keep an eye on him.

"So," Nereus said, "now that we're all ... *friends,* let me explain to you what we'll need and how you can help us. The Ahti are reckless savages, who have purposely followed us here to destroy our otherwise peaceful society."

"Then why do you need our weapons?" asked Minty. "You know, if you're so peaceful."

"I said we are an *otherwise* peaceful society, child," Nereus sneered.

"It's Captain," she replied with a huff.

"*Captain* Minty," he corrected, "I do beg your pardon. But we will do what we must to protect ourselves, and to ensure that our civilization is not extinct. We did not willingly leave Atlantis and all its *treas*—I mean, all its wonderful features, only to be hunted down and exterminated by these ruthless thugs who call themselves merfolk. They are stone-cold killers at best. Much like Captain Sebastian Avery. The one you pulled a flintlock on before you blew him to bits, First Mate Carter."

Carter stood tall, his lean form lengthening. "It was what the situation required," he said.

"Then you understand our predicament perfectly," Nereus countered. "The Okeanos have a long and layered history. We have watched dynasties rise and fall from the depths of our watery realm. We have seen what love, and hate, can do. We have done what we can to make our planet a more tolerable place. But if we do not act, if we do not stand up for ourselves, there will be no one left to stand up for us. We have already fled Atlantis. We will not be forced from these waters as well."

He watched as the three Landers stood quietly, weighing his words.

"Perhaps I can clarify things," said Dorian. "I think the three of you are concerned as to what might happen to your ship. I think we can all agree that it's the most formidable ship we've ever seen. I don't know how you've done it, but the artillery this ship offers, and the scientific research that must've gone into its development, well ... I must say it's impressive beyond belief. Who's the genius behind all that?"

Lyr looked over at Snowy and smiled. "Well," she blushed, "I guess I am."

"That's very flattering," Minty said. "But you still haven't told us how we can help or what we'll need to do. Let's have some answers already."

"Snowy," Lyr said, "you told me about the Kotter cannon. Can you explain to Nereus and Dorian how it works?"

"It has a rapid-fire system, thanks to special rifling," she said, returning his smile. "It allows us to load more ammunition at once and keep firing on our enemies. I learned about it in my cottage in Epping Forest, in England."

"I see," Nereus said. "And we noticed a great deal of bubbles coming from beneath your ship. What causes those?"

"That would be the steam thrusters," Snowy explained. "They can propel us much farther when the need arises."

"Interesting," Nereus said, laying a hand in his icy silver beard. "I imagine we'll need to use all of that."

"What can you tell us about the Ahti?" Carter asked. "After all, *if* we were to help you, we need to know what kind of opposition we're facing."

"That's a fine question, First Mate Carter," Nereus said with a nod. "Dorian?"

"Well," Dorian began, "the Ahti, as Nereus mentioned, are an unscrupulous lot. Barbaric. They threaten any species that they find disagreeable, and they'll try just about anything to intimidate their victims."

"Do they look like you?" Carter inquired. "I mean, how will we be able to identify them? Speaking for the three of us, this is our only face-to-face encounter with merfolk."

"They are slightly larger build," Dorian answered. "Likely due to their voracious appetites. While we wear our hair loose, they wear theirs in plaits. I believe it's some type of tribal custom. And, they often ride kraken."

"Kraken?" Snowy said, her eyes widening. "I thought there was only one, and that it was just a—"

"No, not another myth," Lyr said. "They're real. And there are multitudes of them. Hulking, squid-like beings with fierce yellow eyes and sharp, menacing teeth. If you're not careful, they can swoop you up in their sticky tentacles. And if that happens, there's virtually no escape."

"Sounds like a challenge," Snowy said.

"Which we're not yet ready to accept," said Minty.

Snowy turned to her, frowning. "But they need our help—"

Nereus sat back, amused. If there was one thing he'd learned in all his years leading the Okeanos warriors, it was this: The moment you divide your opposition is the moment you gain an advantage. He stroked his silvery beard and watched the two friends quarrel with each other.

"And we need our ship," Minty replied. "Intact."

"What's the harm of helping someone in need?" Snowy argued.

"What's the harm of sacrificing another ship?" Minty retorted.

"Ladies," Carter said, laying a hand on each of their shoulders, "you obviously have strong opinions. I think it's best that you discuss this further. I mean, it's not like we're going anywhere right now. Nereus and his men won't mind if you take a little time, isn't that right?"

Nereus shook his head, forging his most sincere smile. "Oh, no, of course I won't. You go right ahead."

As they left, Dorian excused himself, saying he needed to check on his troops.

Nereus waved him off and then turned to Lyr.

"Well then," Nereus said. "You've made friends. We're off to a good start. But I don't think Minty is—"

"On board?" Lyr said with a grin.

Nereus dismissed Lyr's pathetic humor with a disappointed groan. "Convinced. Keep working on the blonde one. Once you get her on our side, she'll get the other one to cooperate. I can assure you of that."

{ **seven** }

Snowy drew the corner of her lip upward, shifting her weight as she watched Lyr leave with Nereus. His golden hair swished along his wide shoulders as he moved, much like a dolphin gliding through water. She turned to Minty.

"So, why don't you want to help the Okeanos?"

"I didn't say that I don't want to help them," Minty started. "I'm just hesitant to risk damaging the G2."

"This ship is built for battle," Snowy said.

"So was the original *Gillfish*. Look what happened to her."

"We intentionally sacrificed that first ship," Snowy reminded, elevating her voice.

"While we were still in England," Minty snapped.

"So?"

Minty stamped her foot. "So? So, we're thousands of miles from home. What do we do if we take on damage? Just build another ship out here in the middle of the ocean?"

"We run that risk just by sailing every day," Snowy said. "I don't see any difference."

"And how will we ever get home?" Minty said, a crack in her voice. Carter, who had been standing by quietly, as if afraid to get involved, offered Minty a soft smile.

Snowy started to speak, then paused. "Is that what this is all about? You're homesick?"

Minty drew in a big breath, then let it out, her hands settling in her hair. "I don't know. Maybe? I just … what about Goldie? Don't you want her to be settled? And what about our crew? We've been away for a long time."

"On a great adventure," Snowy replied. "Minty, that's what we do. And in great adventures, we don't always get to determine the course ahead of time. Only God can do that. Sometimes we need to accept the circumstances laid out for us and be flexible enough to adapt."

Carter looked from Snowy to Minty, who shook her head.

"I still don't know," Minty finally said. "I do want to help, but I'm just afraid of the risk. We could lose everything."

"But think of what we could gain," Snowy said. "We could help preserve the Okeanos and keep them safe from the Ahti. Give them peace and freedom. Isn't that worth fighting for?"

"But it's not our fight," Minty urged. "I don't know how you can't see that."

Snowy sighed. "And I don't know how you can't see my side of this."

The three of them stood in silence, eyes shifting randomly, no one willing to look at anyone else.

"I'll tell you what," Snowy said curtly. "I'm going to talk to Lyr and see what else I can find out about the Okeanos and what we can do to help. Why don't you two just … I don't know … check on the crew."

She didn't wait for an answer, just spun on her heel, and made a beeline for the stern. She heard a faint sigh of exasperation behind her as she left.

Lyr was just outside the bubble, at the rail near the gun ports. "Hello, Snowy," he said warmly. "How did it go with your friends?"

Snowy grimaced. "I don't know," she said. "I guess they're still undecided."

Lyr shrugged. "I understand."

"You do?"

"It's a lot to ask, for someone to have faith in something they can't understand."

"I suppose it is," Snowy said, feeling a little more at ease.

"Speaking of things we can't understand, I was hoping you could tell me more about the cannon. Can you show me how it might work?"

"Well, the cannonballs get loaded here," Snowy said, pointing to the back of the Kotter cannon.

"Oh, I know how it works," Lyr said with a laugh. "I'm sorry, I didn't make myself clear. What I mean is, if we are to use it below water to engage the Ahti, how do we use it?"

Snowy squinted at the breech of the cannon. "You know, now that you mention it, I think we have a problem," she said.

"Oh?"

She pushed her glasses up on her nose. "Yes," she said, taking a cannonball from the rack. "See, in order to launch a cannonball under water, we need to create air bubbles, in front of whatever we're launching. Right now, we're in a vacuum."

Lyr blinked.

"That means," Snowy explained, walking as she talked it out to herself, "no air is circulating, which means no oxygen particles are in the breech. And that means these cannonballs will only fly so far when launched. Their inertia will stall, and it will be difficult to guarantee that they'll fly far enough to hit their intended targets. Because the Kotter cannon allows us to fire rapidly, that doesn't do us much good if our shells peter out halfway to their marks. All that does is waste time, energy, gunpowder, and ammunition."

Lyr rested his chin in his hand and looked her up and down. "Fascinating," he said. "Tell me, how did you learn so much?"

"I like to read," Snowy giggled. "Most people think it's weird, but I've just always loved reading and learning and exploring, especially when it comes to science. I know it's odd. Most girls aren't like this."

"You're obviously not like most girls, Snowy," he said with a lingering look.

She caught herself staring at him and then turned her attention back to the cannon. "No. No, I suppose I'm not," she said. "So ... um, I think what I need to figure out is a way ... "

"But Snowy," Lyr said, "you should know that you're actually not in a vacuum. You see, thanks to Fiz, we have harnessed oxygen for you in our amphorae."

"Amph-or-what?" she asked, confused.

"Vases, Snowy," Lyr clarified. "I explained how you have the personal air pot. See how they have the five bubbles on them?"

Snowy looked at the little pot hanging near her waist and ran her fingers over the carving. It was, in fact, five small circles.

"Yes?"

"That means they carry oxygen," Lyr said. "And you have the oxidators for your heads. If you could see down below the ship, you'd see that we have placed two very large amphorae below it. We pull them into place with sea turtles. They generate the oxygen necessary to create the bubble over the ship."

"Oh, of course," Snowy said, realizing she'd forgotten about the bubble. "That makes sense now."

"And if you'll look behind you," Lyr said with a charming smile, "you'll see that we also placed one on the deck to provide clean, dry air so that all of you Landers can breathe without the oxidators."

She turned and looked. Sure enough, there was a very large vase, brilliant blue with wavy lines marked on it, sitting near the ship's wheel. It seemed odd that she hadn't noticed it before, but between being captivated by Lyr, and bickering with Minty about helping the Okeanos, Snowy forgave herself for being so distracted and unobservant.

"Ah, very clever," she said. "So, if that's the case, then we *can* fire our cannons. But I'm worried about breaking the bubble."

"I suppose that's a risk we must take," Lyr said. "As I've said, any hole the projectiles make should seal itself back up immediately, but there's no guarantee."

Snowy frowned.

"But that's why you have the oxidators," Lyr reminded. "You'll still be safe."

"I'm just afraid that something will go wrong, and the ship might sink, even if we can breathe underwater," she said. "I'm not sure how we'd navigate."

The speckles on Lyr's face came together as he shrugged, but his eyes were still warm and friendly. Snowy watched him float back and forth in the water, his gills rising and falling, and his glimmering tail swishing gently from side to side. She was drawn to him, and instinctively moved closer to the bubble. He leaned toward her, placing a webbed hand against the barrier. She raised her hand to meet it, feeling a faint ray of warmth emanating from the bubble. After a few moments, he backed away, as two mermen on squid and a family of sea turtles swam behind him.

"Wait a minute," Snowy said, shaking her head as the idea sank in. "Are there more of these air pots?"

"Yes, Fiz is constantly making these," Lyr said. "He tests them for a multitude of functions, experiments with their contents, and creates them in varying sizes. He's too old and frail to fight alongside us anymore. I've heard that he was once a very strong and capable warrior. But now that his fighting days are over, he makes a considerable contribution to our defensive capabilities with his scientific knowledge."

"He sounds fascinating. I'd love to meet him sometime," Snowy said. "And I'm going to need another one of these big amph—what did you call them?"

"*Amphorae*," Lyr said.

"Yes, those. I'm going to need one of those, a really big one, to put down in the steam chamber, below deck," Snowy said. "With our sails down and useless underwater, it'll create enough air pressure to propel the *G2* while submerged, if we need it. You think Fiz will lend us one for that?"

"Probably," Lyr said, "but I'll warn you, he's not really the friendly sort."

"You mean, he's not like you?" Snowy asked with a coy smile.

Lyr laughed. "I suppose not," he said. "But I bet you'll charm him, like you've charmed me, with your scientific knowledge."

"That's it!" Snowy exclaimed. She reached into the pocket of her dress and pulled out a small notebook and a pen, furiously scribbling numbers and sketching out shapes.

"What are you doing?"

"Solving our problem," she said, her jaw set as she worked the equation. "There!"

She held up the notebook to show Lyr, but he just shook his head slowly.

"I'm sorry, I don't understand what it means," he said with a shrug.

"In order for these cannonballs to fly further under water, we need air bubbles. So, we need to create a small charge of gunpowder ahead of the cannonball," she clarified. "Then, we need to use the regular, larger load of gunpowder behind the cannonball."

Lyr just stared. "Sure," he said, but his confused look indicated that he really didn't follow.

Snowy smirked, "Trust me, it'll work."

"Good," he said, "because I wouldn't even know what questions to ask."

She was proud of herself for figuring out a way to battle the Ahti, assuming Minty came to her senses. And Lyr seemed very sincere. She was enjoying spending time with him.

"Now," she said, "I have a question for you."

"I hope it's not about cannons or gunpowder or vacuums," he said.

"No," Snowy laughed. "Nothing like that, I promise. I'm tired of talking about that stuff." She noticed the gauzy webbing between his fingers, and the shimmering blue scales that led up his arm. It was so unusual, and she was surprised that it didn't bother her.

He leaned closer, pressing against the bubble until it began to give. "What did you want to ask?"

Snowy glanced up, looking at his speckled-blue face. "What's the Eye of India?"

{ **eight** }

Minty sighed as she walked with Carter to her cabin. It was a quiet place to think things through.

"You want some tea?" she asked.

Carter shook his head as he stretched his lanky frame over the small chair in the corner, folded up like an ironing board. "No, thank you."

"How about a muffin?"

He looked around the tiny space, eyes drifting from photographs to books to the silver hairbrush on her petite vanity table.

"Uh, no," he said. "I'm fine."

Minty plopped herself on the edge of the bed, facing Carter, and tore into the muffin she'd intended to eat for breakfast, hours ago. The scents of cinnamon and vanilla soothed her foul mood. She closed her eyes, grunting softly as she chewed. "I don't know what to do," she began. "I don't feel like we can trust these mermen and it's as if Snowy doesn't understand the danger we might be in."

Carter nodded. "Well, maybe that's because they don't seem dangerous to her."

"I don't get it," Minty said. "Why wouldn't she think they're dangerous? Did you see Dorian? And Nereus? There's something suspicious about him. He gave me the creeps. Why doesn't Snowy see that?"

Carter shifted in the little chair and it creaked. Then he sat up straight, as if afraid to move. "Because she's only looking at Lyr," he said.

Minty stared at Carter, whose eyes widened. "Why would she only be looking at—"

Carter smiled and slowly nodded his head.

Minty sat back, the realization washing over her like a sunbeam warming her freckled skin in Epping. "Oh … OH."

How am I just now realizing this?

"He has clearly made an impression on her," Carter said.

"I guess he has," Minty said, nibbling at the muffin more daintily now that she could see things from a different perspective. "But … wow … I just, I didn't even think of that. She has a crush on him."

"Or maybe they're just … infatuated," Carter offered.

Minty brushed the crumbs from her mouth and twirled her fingers through her hair, aimlessly spinning the tendrils along her shoulders. "What do you mean?"

"You know," Carter said, looking down at the floor, "like how sometimes, you just really enjoy spending time with someone. You look forward to seeing them every day so you can learn more about what they like. Maybe, uh, maybe you like the way their hair smells."

Minty laughed. "I can't even imagine what a merman's hair must smell like."

Carter cleared his throat, letting out a weak laugh as he shifted again in the creaky chair. "Oh, me neither. Probably like stinky seaweed."

"Or clams," Minty said, shoving the last of the muffin into her mouth. "Gross."

Carter laughed again. "Yeah, gross."

When their laughter died down, Minty said, "I still don't know what to do. I really want to trust them, and Snowy made a good point about having faith. But I'm so afraid of risking the G2. What would we do if something happened?"

"Well," Carter said, finally settling into a more comfortable position, "let's think about it this way: What are your biggest hesitations?"

"Hm," Minty said, resting her chin in her hand as she leaned toward Carter. "It's scary but if anything happens, I think we can fix the ship."

"Really?"

"Sure, we've done it before. And I do want to get home to Epping, but, Snowy's right. This is a once-in-a-lifetime adventure. You know, I miss my family, even though they're gone." Minty felt dampness in the corners of her eyes, and it surprised her.

Carter reached into his shirt pocket and gave her a handkerchief, embroidered in dark blue. NEC.

She wiped her eyes. "Thank you," she said. "What does the E stand for?"

"Oh, it's embarrassing," he said, shaking his head. "My mother, from what I remember, she—"

"That's right," Minty said, "you don't have any family, either."

"No," he said. "Not for a long time. But ... tell me, what's your biggest concern with letting the Okeanos use the *G2*?"

Minty folded the handkerchief into a neat square and set it on her lap. "I guess I just don't trust Nereus," she said. "I feel like he's trying to hide something. And maybe Lyr and the rest of them don't know it."

"Huh," Carter said, stretching out again. "That's interesting because, to be honest, I get that feeling, too. There's something odd about him, isn't there?"

"YES!" Minty bolted up, letting Carter's handkerchief fall to the floor. "Remember when he was talking about Atlantis? And he started to say—"

"TREASURE," Carter chimed in.

"Yes, you heard that, too?"

"I did," Carter said, bending down to retrieve his handkerchief and stuffing it in his shirt pocket.

"Yeah, what would he care about treasure? And where would he keep it anyway?"

"Right. So ... what do you want to do?"

"Well," Minty said, walking over to her little vanity table where she began brushing her hair, "I don't think we have much choice, to be honest. I think we'll have to cooperate. We are technically their prisoners. And I do want to help save them from the Ahti. But ... "

She let the brush go through the length of her long, wavy locks, then stopped, catching a glimpse of Carter behind her in her vanity mirror.

"But what?"

She spun around and pointed her brush at Carter. "But I think we need to learn more about Nereus."

"I'm all in for that," he said, standing up.

"Snowy won't like it," Minty said with a frown, setting the brush on her vanity table.

"So? Who said she has to know?"

Minty smiled. "Exactly."

"So, how do you want to do this?"

Minty pushed her hair back and smoothed her dress as she looked over her shoulder and into the mirror. "You start talking to Dorian, see what you can learn. If he's not much of a talker, maybe move on to some of the lower-ranked soldiers."

"The ones on the seahorses?"

"Exactly," Minty said. "And, I'm going to see what I can find out from the ones who ride the squids."

"Sounds like a plan," Carter said, stepping toward the door.

Minty crossed the room and Carter turned the knob. "There's just one more thing," she said.

"What?"

She straightened the handkerchief in Carter's pocket, then patted it with her hand. "Tell me what the E stands for."

He smiled and pushed the door open, holding it open for her. Then with a teasing chuckle, he said, "Nope, not today."

***

"The Eye of India," Lyr said, his words trailing off as he leaned closer to Snowy.

Even through the bubble, she detected that he had a soft aroma about him, like sunlight hitting the water on a quiet summer morning. It seemed to trail through his hair. She inhaled as his amber eyes scanned the *G2*'s deck for anyone who might overhear. Then he turned to her.

"The Eye of India," he repeated slowly, "is one of the most breathtaking treasures anyone has ever seen."

"I've never heard of it," Snowy said, focusing on the blue speckles that swooped upward along Lyr's strong cheekbones, fading into his golden hairline.

"Captain Avery seized it from the Okeanos about ten years ago," Lyr explained.

"Oh?" Snowy was caught off guard. "What is it, a jewel? I know he liked to use them in his cutlass."

"Well," Lyr said, looking over his shoulder at his fellow mermen going about their duties behind him, "technically, but not exactly."

Snowy cocked her head. "Then what is it?"

Lyr inhaled. "You must keep this to yourself. The Eye of India is extremely valuable to the Okeanos. It is a massive, rare blue pearl, gleaming and bright and perfectly formed. It was a gift from the Pacificans."

"The Pacificans? Who are they?"

"A distant tribe of mermen," Lyr confided. "They gifted it to Nereus as a token of appreciation, many years ago, for helping them in their time of need."

"And Captain Avery took it?"

Lyr nodded.

"That's interesting," Snowy said, watching Lyr's face for an indicator that he wasn't being truthful, but there wasn't one. "Because when we took over Avery's ships, we impounded all the treasure that was aboard. We gave some to the people of Bridgetown, to cover the costs of Avery's pirates, who are now helping defend the island, and help their economy in general. I looked through all the loot, but I don't recall any pearls among the treasure we confiscated, especially not one like you just described."

"Well, here's something else you need to keep to yourself," he said, his voice lowered to a whisper.

Snowy held her breath. "What's that?"

"I think Nereus has it," Lyr said.

"Why do you—" Snowy blurted out, then continued in a whisper, "why do you think that? Have you seen it?"

Lyr shook his head, then quickly pulled away from the bubble as a pair of mermaids went by, each giggling as they cradled merbabies.

Snowy straightened her shoulders and watched the mermaids pass, giving them a faint smile. Then she turned back to Lyr, eyes widened.

"I haven't seen it," Lyr explained. "But, Nereus went off by himself after Avery's ship was destroyed. Dorian went to find him. He felt it was important for Nereus to address the troops as soon as possible, and he had disappeared."

"And?" Snowy asked, incredulous.

"And," Lyr said, "when Dorian found him, Nereus was acting strange. You see, he's always resented Avery for taking the Eye of India, and for the way he took it. The story I heard is that Avery came across Nereus swimming one day and chased him with his ship, pinning him into a narrow inlet. He was rather cruel."

"So I've heard," Snowy said, shuddering to think of some of the awful stories she'd been told about Sebastian Avery over the years.

"Oh, you have no idea," Lyr continued, again leaning toward her from outside the bubble. "I won't go into some of the atrocities we've heard about. No need to upset you with those."

"Thank you," she said. "So, what happened with Nereus? How did he escape?"

"Well," Lyr said, "you probably know enough about Avery to know he was a sick man. That is, he really enjoyed torturing others. Much like the Ahti, come to think of it. In fact, I suspect they may have had an alliance, because it seemed that they both followed us from Atlantis."

"Hm," Snowy mused. "Could be."

"Anyway, Avery wanted to terrorize Nereus, just for the fun of it. So, for more than an hour, he chased him, cutting off his escape path, exhausting him and threatening to capture him. Said he'd make a fine prize and would have him mounted and hung over the desk in his quarters."

"Ugh," Snowy said, her stomach clenching at the thought. "That's terrible."

"It was," Lyr continued. "Nereus is very proud. He has served as our leader for decades. But he was broken that day, and terrified. Avery could've killed him right away, but instead he chose to torment him. And in the end, he made Nereus beg for his life, stripping him of his dignity. And then, just to toy with him, Avery made a bargain with him—his life for the Eye of India."

"Oh, wow," Snowy said, scanning the sea for Nereus. He was in the distance, talking to Dorian, looking very leaderlike, strong and broad-shouldered, enriched with the wisdom borne of numerous battles. With his comportment, she had a hard time picturing him groveling and imploring Captain Avery to spare his life.

"Right," Lyr said, "so, Nereus led Avery and his ship back to our colony, where he retrieved the Eye of India and surrendered it. Just like that. No discussion, no argument, no resistance. He just gave it up. No one really talked about it. I mean, there were whispers among the lower-ranking officers. But everyone understood. Nereus had been humiliated. And it took a while for him to regain our respect."

Snowy nodded wistfully. "And you think he somehow acquired the Eye of India after we destroyed Avery's ship?"

"I think it's very likely," Lyr said. "Like I said, Dorian mentioned that Nereus went off by himself for a while. He swam in the direction of the battle, where one of Avery's ships was blown apart. Not too far from here, now that I think of it. And when he came back, he seemed nervous, but also sort of calm. You know what I mean?"

Snowy shrugged. "No, not really. Sorry."

"He seemed *happy*," Lyr said.

"I think if I were him, I'd be happy about Avery being gone, too," Snowy reasoned.

"Maybe. But, Snowy, Nereus is *never* happy. About anything. We've had victories before, defeated enemies, had wonderful achievements, prospered as a species. But he's never been anything but stoic."

"Well, that is odd, then," she concluded.

"Dorian said he was humming and smiling after he came back," Lyr explained. "And when Dorian asked him about it, Nereus suddenly got angry, telling Dorian to mind his business and to never spy on him again."

"Was he spying?"

"I don't think so," Lyr said. "I think he just didn't realize Nereus was there, and it surprised them both."

Snowy pushed her glasses up her nose. "Weird. So, you think he's got the Eye of India stashed away?"

"Somewhere on the ocean floor, yes," Lyr said.

"Why wouldn't he just tell the Okeanos that he has it? What's the benefit in keeping it to himself?"

"Well," Lyr said, again checking for eavesdroppers, "that's a bit of a mystery. But, my best guess is that he recognizes its value as a bargaining chip."

"Like he used it to negotiate for his life with Avery," Snowy surmised. "Interesting."

"But now, we're dealing with the Ahti, who are cold-blooded killers," Lyr said. "And I assure you they'd rather see us all dead than negotiate for any kind of treasure."

Snowy let that idea sink in, then looked at Lyr. "You know what? We're going to help you."

Lyr smiled, his gills ruffling and his blue speckles glinting in the light. "You are? But what about Minty? She didn't seem very willing—"

"She will be," Snowy said, putting her hand up to Lyr's against the bubble. "But we want something in return."

"You name it, Snowy."

"Well, two things, actually," she began. "First, we'll help you fight the Ahti in exchange for our freedom."

"Of course," Lyr said. "That's not even a question. What's the other thing?"

Snowy tucked a strand of hair behind her ear. "We want the Eye of India."

Lyr drew back. "Oh, I don't know if—"

But before he could finish, the *G2*'s hull shook violently, tossing Snowy against the bubble. She felt Lyr shield her with his blue-speckled body as shouts and screams came from the deck.

"We're under attack!" Dorian yelled from the saddle of his seahorse, swimming toward the ship. "Prepare for battle!"

{ nine }

"What was that?" Minty yelled, her boots thudding up the steps to the deck as the G2 rocked back and forth. Carter fell in behind her and the crew began manning their stations.

"Kraken!" she heard someone shout.

As the G2 trembled, she nearly tripped over a big blue piece of pottery. Once she steadied herself, she grasped the ship's wheel, desperate to hold onto something solid. But she quickly realized it didn't matter. Her ship was trapped in this air bubble, an easy target. They couldn't get away, and she was afraid to fire. All they could do was sit there, defenseless, and pray they survived the attack.

"Look!" Carter said, pointing to something dark and shadowy moving off the starboard side.

Minty turned and saw an enormous, eight-armed creature, thrashing from side to side. On its back sat a pale blue merman, his dark hair arranged in long, tight braids trailing down his broad back.

"What are your orders, Captain?" Clem shouted.

Minty stared in disbelief at the giant octopus-like creature, still in awe of its size.

"Captain Minty?" Rogers chimed in.

"Hold your positions!" Minty yelled.

What can we do? If only we hadn't gone back to Bridgetown, this never would've happened.

Goldie's screams jolted Minty out of her thoughts. This was no time for self-pity. She had to think about others.

And then, just as suddenly as it began, the shaking stopped.

Minty spun and looked to the starboard side, only to see the kraken's tentacles flailing in the water upon releasing the *G2*. The burly merman on its back appeared to laugh. Then he pointed to Nereus and Dorian, who were clustered with their troops, and saluted as if to say, "See you soon."

Clem scooped up Goldie and patted her back, comforting her until she stopped crying.

"Was that what I think it was?" Snowy said, approaching the ship's wheel.

"Kraken," Carter announced. Then he looked back at Minty. "You all right?"

Minty nodded and exhaled. "Yes, thank you." Then she turned to Snowy. "Where were you?"

"I was with Lyr, learning more about the Okeanos," she explained. "They really need our help."

"I think we can see that," Minty said with an air of dismissiveness.

"Good, because I told him that we'd help," Snowy retorted.

"You wha—" Minty started, then paused. "You know what? It doesn't matter. Let's just do this and get it over with. Although I don't know how we're going to help if all we can do is sit here." She let out a loud huff and shook her head.

"I'm working on that," Snowy said, holding up her notebook and flipping to a page with equations scribbled all the way down and a cannon diagram. "I'm not done yet, but I've started to figure it out."

Carter looked at the notebook and nodded. "You know, I think this might work," he said. "Minty, it'll be fine. We can work with Nereus to help them fight the Ahti."

Minty softened her glare at Carter's words. "But I told you," she whispered. "I don't trust Nereus."

Snowy stepped toward Minty, "I'm not sure I do, either. Especially after what Lyr said."

Minty raised a brow. "Oh, really?"

Snowy, speaking in hushed tones, relayed the gist of what Lyr had told her, that they suspected Nereus was concealing a valuable piece of Captain Avery's captured treasure.

Minty stood quietly for a moment, eyes drifting toward Nereus, Dorian, and Lyr, who were conferring with their troops on the seahorses. "Interesting," she said, her thoughts churning. Then she turned to Snowy. "How long do you think it'll take to work out the formula for firing the cannon?"

"Hard to say. I think I'm close, but the biggest obstacle is that we can't do any test fires," Snowy said. "I have to rely on the math, and some of it is just guesswork."

"Hm," Minty said, finally feeling a sense of calm. "What other options do we have for defending ourselves?"

"Again, hard to say," Snowy shrugged. "I've got to figure that out, too. This air bubble is keeping us alive, but it's almost limiting our options. Wish I could call in a favor from the Royal Observatory right now."

Minty watched Dorian and Nereus, paying close attention to their movements. It seemed that whenever Nereus spoke, he tilted his head back and looked past Dorian. As Nereus' silvery locks brushed the middle of his back, Dorian leaned away from him.

"Carter," Minty said, eyes still on the Okeanos leader, "help Snowy with whatever she needs. Get as many crew members as you can to figure out a strategy. I'll be back in a little bit."

"Sure," Carter said as Minty strode off.

Let's see if my hunch is right.

"Nereus," Minty said, approaching him and rapping against the bubble until he swam over. "Is everyone all right?"

"Yes," he said. "We were lucky this time. But I'm sure you can see why we need your ship and its resources to fight these vicious savages."

"And you'll have it," Minty said. "We are at your disposal. Snowy is figuring out the specifics so that we can use the cannons underwater."

"Very well, Captain Minty," Nereus said with a mock bow, his tail swishing as he did so. "I knew you'd see it our way, once you realized what was at stake. Tell me, was that your first encounter with a kraken?"

"Yes," Minty said.

"And what did you think? Terrifying, isn't it?"

Minty stared at him, unwilling to show her fear. "I suppose," she said with a shrug.

Nereus placed his webbed hands behind his back. "Well," he said, "that wasn't the reaction I was expecting."

Minty looked at Dorian and motioned for him to come over. "Can I borrow you for a moment?" she asked. "I think we'll need to discuss strategy."

Dorian looked to Nereus, his pale green gills fluttering.

"Go ahead," Nereus said. "I have a few things to check on."

"Thank you," Minty said as Nereus swam off. Then she turned to Dorian.

"So, Captain Minty," he said, "what did you have in mind?"

"What do you know about the Eye of India?" she said, getting straight to the point.

"The ... who told you ... "

Minty crossed her arms. "Look, with all due respect, I don't know how much time we have before Nereus comes back, or the Ahti, for that matter. There's no time for questions right now. We're going to help you, but I need you to make me a promise, and Nereus can't know about it."

Dorian sighed, then he looked around.

"He's talking to the soldiers on the seahorses," she said. "He can't hear us."

"So," Dorian said, "what do you want?"

Minty leaned closer. "I need you to make me a promise, for something that may happen in the future. It's important that you agree."

Dorian blinked. "What do you mean?"

Minty caught sight of Nereus, who was working his way back toward them but still out of earshot. She turned her eyes again to Dorian. "I'm going to need you to do us a favor."

***

Snowy was anxious about meeting Fiz. Lyr had said he wasn't very friendly. She hoped that wouldn't be an obstacle as she waited for him to swim up to the ship.

It wasn't long before Lyr swam up to the bubble, with a small, withered merman trailing behind him.

"Snowy," Lyr said. "This is Fiz, our bubble master and an esteemed elder in our society."

"Pleased to meet you," Snowy said, instinctively holding out her hand until she realized he couldn't shake it. "Thank you for coming up to meet me."

Fiz had steely blue-grey eyes, nearly the same color as his skin. In fact, except for his pure white hair and beard, everything about him was the color of a storm-splattered sky. He glared at her, his gills moving slowly as he bobbed in the water. Finally, he nodded to acknowledge her.

"Well," Snowy said, "Lyr tells me you've experimented with the amphorae as to what kinds of gases they can hold."

Again, he nodded without speaking.

"Great," Snowy said, wondering if he would ever say anything, "that's great. So, uh, I'm wondering if we can borrow another of the large amphorae for oxygen. I need, I mean, I'd like to put it in our steam chamber below deck. This will allow us to propel the ship and—"

"You use steam thrusters?" Fiz asked in a thin, weak voice.

"Yes! Steam thrusters, exactly," Snowy said with a smile.

"You have one," Fiz said, his frail body barely moving. With labored breath, he continued, "We moved one into place near the boiler for such an occasion."

Snowy's eyes widened. "We do? You did?"

"Yes," he said, nearly gasping. "It's down there. With your sails down, you'll be able to move through the water easily."

"Oh, thank you! I guess I hadn't noticed," she said. "I must say, that was great foresight."

The thin little merman shrugged. "I've seen enough in my time," he said, his tiny frame beginning to soften from its rigid posture. "When Nereus was a boy, his father, Phirun, liked to experiment with gases and steam. The two of us made it a hobby. That was a long time ago. But I never gave it up. I knew when I saw your ship that you'd need that oxygen pot once he brought it down here."

Snowy and Lyr exchanged a glance.

"So, you've seen our ship before?" she asked.

He let out a wheezing cough. "Sure," he said, his eyes beginning to brighten to a crisper shade of blue. "Well, I sensed it. You see, I keep to myself on the ocean floor, mostly. But I can detect the different vibrations of sea life. Each one is unique. When your ship passed by, I took note of the different reverberations. I hear you used it to defeat Captain Avery."

"We did indeed," Snowy said.

"Good," Fiz said. "He was a jerk."

"OH!" Snowy said, unexpectedly letting out a little laugh. "So, Fiz, what other hobbies do you have? Any other experiments you like to do?"

He slowly swam closer to the edge of the bubble. For the first time, Snowy noticed how much he reminded her of her grandfather. Even though it had been years since she'd seen him, there was something about Fiz that comforted her, the way her grandfather did on dark nights in the observatory as he scratched out equations while they looked at the stars.

"This is sort of in development," he began, "but there's a lava tube straight down from this side of the ship."

"Lava tube?" Snowy asked, intrigued.

"Yes, and my workshop is right there at its edge."

"Ooh, you have a workshop!" Snowy squealed, rubbing her hands together with excitement. "I wish I could take a look."

"I'm afraid you wouldn't survive that far below the surface," Lyr interjected. "Even with the oxidator."

Snowy frowned. "Oh well," she said. "Fiz, tell me what your workshop is like."

"It's where I experiment with all the different elements like hydrogen," he explained. "I used a hose from the hydrogen tank to sink your ship, actually. But I keep various gases in different tanks."

"Interesting," Snowy said. "Not long ago, we used methane from tanks to create an explosion and rescue children from the factory of an evil man who makes telescopes."

Lyr and Fiz both blinked at Snowy, their faces utterly blank.

"Well," Fiz said after a brief silence, his warped little hands gesturing, "when the molten lava bubbles up, I've been playing around with using an apparatus to harness the steam."

"Which must result from the water bubbling against the lava," Snowy reasoned.

"Exactly. And then I use a turbine. It creates some sort of energy that I can't explain. And there are certain creatures that are attracted to it. I'm not sure why. But I'm still working on it."

"Sounds fascinating," Snowy said, thoroughly charmed by this merman she was expecting to be gruff and unfriendly.

"It's good to chat with someone who understands," he said. "You see, I ... I have this theory about underwater volcanoes and ..." His voice trailed off as he looked over his shoulder.

Snowy leaned against the bubble so that she could be as close to Fiz as possible. "And?"

His gills fluttered as he built up the strength to speak. "Eels."

***

Later, down in her cabin, Snowy rifled through her notebooks, thinking about the theory Fiz had described and more. There was so much to figure out still and she was afraid that there wouldn't be enough time.

"Kraken, kraken, kraken … " she mused aloud.

"Hi," said Carter, knocking on the door and poking his head in. "I hope you don't mind. I wanted to check on you."

"No, come in," Snowy said, clearing a little room on the table. "Sit down. You can help me."

"Help you with what?" he asked, looking at the jumbled pile of notebooks on the table.

"I'm trying to learn more about kraken," she said, her head down as she pushed a trio of notebooks toward him. "Take one of these and see if you can find anything."

"And what am I looking for?"

Snowy looked up. "Anything," she said. "If I recall correctly, I jotted it down in one of these books. I just can't remember which one. There are illustrations, if that helps."

"Like this?" Carter said, turning a notebook around and pointing to a drawing of a large octopus-like creature.

"Yes!" Snowy grabbed the notebook. "That's it!"

Carter drew back.

"Sorry," Snowy said, aware she had acted rudely. "I'm just … anxious, I guess. I've never had to battle kraken or mermen before."

"Makes two of us," Carter quipped.

"And, I've certainly never had to fight anything while trapped in a big bubble," Snowy said. "I think I have all the cannon trajectory figured out and how to adjust the gunpowder dosage. At least, I hope I do. But, there are a lot of factors to consider and I'm so afraid I'm missing something. That's why I need to learn everything I can about the kraken before the Ahti return. We need to be ready to help Lyr—er, the *Okeanos*—even though I know Minty doesn't agree."

Carter raised a brow. "You seem to be quite friendly with Lyr."

"He's a good person," Snowy said, "or, merman, I guess. I'm not sure how to refer to him, to be honest. He's funny and caring and it seems like he has similar values."

Carter paused. "Sounds like a good person," he said with a smile. "But, what about Nereus? Minty said she doesn't trust him."

"Well, there's something we do agree on," Snowy said, starting to sketch in the notebook as she spoke. "Look, I feel like she's mad at me, and maybe you are, too. But I want you to be sure that whatever we do, I intend to protect the *G2* at all costs. So, I'm trying to figure out how to escape if necessary."

"I don't think anyone's mad at you," Carter assured. "I think she was confused but not anymore. The two of you should talk it out, though."

"I'm sure you're right."

"Now, more than once, the Okeanos have said they mean us no harm," Carter noted. "Do you believe that?"

Snowy looked up. "I suppose that depends on which of the Okeanos is telling me that."

"Exactly," Carter nodded. "And I think we're all in agreement, if I may speak for Minty. So, now that that's settled, what can I do to help you? What do you need?"

"Well, I was just thinking of something to help the ship move through the water in an emergency," she said. "I'm going to get one of those big air pots for the steam chamber since we can't use our sails. That should help propel us. But I also need to learn more about kraken, and I can't draw or calculate and read at the same time.

Could you read that information on kraken to me while I try to figure this out?"

"Of course," Carter said. He looked through the notebook entry and then began. "It says they're rumored to be seen in the North Atlantic."

"Well, they've made their way south, haven't they?" Snowy said, working on a sketch.

Carter chuckled. "I'd say so. Let's see. It also talks about their size."

"Huge."

"Right. And their teeth."

"Big and sharp, got it."

"Yes," Carter said. "Oh, and this is interesting. And, gross."

"What's that?"

"Due to their enormous size, it says that when they eat, they … hm, no polite way to say this, I'm afraid, but they belch in order to attract large quantities of fish."

"Really? That would not attract me in any way."

"Right, don't put me down for being eaten by kraken," Carter laughed.

"Likewise," Snowy chuckled, grateful that Carter had lightened the mood.

"And then," Carter continued, "all the fish gather because they believe they'll be fed."

Snowy looked up. "Now how would anyone know that? Did they ask the fish?"

"I'm just reading what it says," Carter said. "So, let's see, the fish gather and swim into the kraken's mouth."

"Bet that smells good."

"Right? And then once the kraken's mouth and stomach have filled, it locks its jaws, trapping them all inside."

"Ugh, yuck," Snowy said, making a face. "That is gross."

"I told you," Carter said, his fingers running over the pages. "Now, here's something else. This says that they stay on the sea floor for days at a time between feedings, sometimes mistaken for islands, and then burst to the surface."

"That much I knew," Snowy said, scribbling an equation.

"But, the biggest danger isn't so much being eaten by the kraken."

"Really? Because that sounds somewhat dangerous."

"Yes, but it says that being caught in the whirlpool left from its wake can be more deadly."

Snowy cocked her head and nodded. "Duly noted. Let's avoid that."

"Definitely," Carter said, thumbing through the notebook. "And it looks like that's about it."

Snowy looked at her sketches and checked her math. Then she doodled some more. "Now," she said, "I need to do some research on a way to get these amphorae—"

"Am-what?"

Snowy laughed. "Amphorae," she said, as if she'd known what it meant for years. "Vases. The Okeanos have a bubble master named Fiz—"

"Catchy," Carter grinned.

"Right," Snowy said, sketching out a series of vases in her notebook and marking them with symbols. "So, he spends a lot of time working on these amphorae, experimenting with how to fill them with air and create bubbles."

"Like our steam thrusters create bubbles?"

"Sort of," Snowy said, holding the notebook up and showing him. "See, they used two of them to create enough oxygen to release the bubble that's protecting the ship. And they put one on the deck near the wheel, to provide fresh air for us to breathe, so we don't have to use the oxidators."

"I saw that," Carter said. "Was wondering what that was, but it was a little, you know, hectic. What with being attacked by a kraken and all."

"Exactly," Snowy said. "And there's one down in the steam chamber, which will help us propel the ship underwater."

"Oh, that will be helpful," Carter said. "Did you think of that?"

"No, Fiz did, actually. They put it in place when they sunk the ship, apparently. And, this is weird, but he says he's seen our ship before, and *sensed* it."

"Sensed?"

"Yes, he has this odd, heightened sort of intuition, I guess you'd call it."

Carter nodded.

"So," Snowy said, drawing in her notebook, "we have these little vases for our own air supply, and these very large vases to provide oxygen to the ship. Now, they used one of these to pull us down here. The force was that powerful."

"I see," Carter said, looking over the vases she'd sketched. "But what do these symbols mean?"

Snowy pointed to her drawings, "The pot with the five bubbles is oxygen, and the pot with the three bubbles and flames is hydrogen. I'm thinking, there are volcanoes down here, right? If we can harness the power of a volcano to break up seawater somehow, and separate it into hydrogen and oxygen, we'll be well-equipped to fight the Ahti."

Carter nodded. "Snowy, I don't know how you do it, but that's brilliant."

"Thank you, Carter," she said. "But I did have a little help."

He leaned back in the chair and smiled. "So, what do you know about the Ahti?"

"The same things you know," Snowy said. "They're heartless killers, who are bigger and stronger than the Okeanos, and they ride kraken."

"So, no particular strategy when it comes to fighting them?"

Snowy shook her head. "They have the size advantage, and it sounds like there are more of them, so ... we just have to be smarter."

Carter tilted his head to get a better look at her equations.

"Well then," he said. "If that's the case, I think we'll be fine."

Snowy sat back in her chair and rubbed her temples. All those calculations in such a short span of time, not to mention her discussion with Fiz earlier, had worn her out. But there was no time to rest. Her brain was overflowing with information, and she couldn't be sure she'd thought of everything. Most of all, she hoped that Fiz was right about his theory. With a sigh, she said, "I hope so."

{ ten }

Nereus gazed into the murky depths, his pale amber eyes drifting to where the massive kraken had swum off with the Ahti merman on its back. His long, silvery hair puffed intermittently over his gills as he watched, deep in thought. The Ahti would be back. There was no doubt about that. The only thing in question was whether the Okeanos would've done enough to prepare when those blood-thirsty thugs showed up.

He closed his eyes, recalling a time when things were much simpler. He'd grown up in abundance, the only son of a wealthy aristocrat who was highly respected among the Okeanos. His father, Phirun, was sixty when Nereus was born, much more mature than most new fathers. Nereus' mother, Tethys, was only twenty, but had died in childbirth, Phirun said. From then on, it had been just the two of them. And although they didn't always agree on everything, they each understood their role in their binary family unit. They inhabited a well-equipped cave, perched high within the vast underwater canyons of Atlantis, with several young mermaids to serve them. Spoiled, Nereus never lacked anything. In fact, if he ever wanted something, he simply took it. As such, he developed a taste for fine things such as rare, exotic corals, polished tortoise shells, and the ocean's most precious gems—dazzling pearls.

Nereus moved through Atlantan society with ease, always saying the right thing at the right time, impressing those who made important decisions for the Okeanos population, and charming the loveliest mermaids with luxurious gifts.

But by the age of twenty-five, he'd grown bored, and increasingly resentful of his father, who had become less supportive of Nereus' cavalier lifestyle in his old age.

"You're wasting your life," Phirun scolded one day, having returned home from a government conference to find Nereus lounging about the cave. "When I was your age, I'd already made something of myself."

"What do you know?" a young Nereus retorted. "You're old and feeble now."

Phirun swam over and pressed himself against Nereus' chest. "I'm still your father, the only parent who cared enough to stay."

Nereus drew back. "What do you mean by that? My mother died. She didn't have a choice."

"It's time you knew the truth," Phirun snarled. "Your mother didn't die giving birth to you. She went back to her people, and we're all better for it."

Nereus' mouth fell open. "Wait, she's alive? And what do you mean she 'went back to her people?' Here in Atlantis?"

Phirun choked back a deep cough, gasping as he explained. "Your mother is something ... less than an Atlantan. She's an Ahti. She schemed and tricked her way into getting me to marry her, hoping my wealth would keep her comfortable. She was lazy, and although I've done my best to raise you to be responsible, you're just like her."

Nereus quivered in disbelief. His own father had lied to him for twenty-five years about something so critical, the very core of his identity. With no mother to nurture him, he'd found comfort in fancy things. But it was all a lie.

That was the night he left and joined the Atlantan military. He was torn between a father who didn't want him and a mother he didn't know. He wasn't sure how to feel about her, whether he should try to find her, or if he should just let her be. So he focused his energy on military training, working his body into a strong, fit machine capable of defeating any enemy.

He quickly worked his way up the ranks, impressing his commanding officers and gaining the trust and respect of the enlisted men, despite his privileged background. Still, Ruarc, the military's grand commander, challenged him. It seemed Ruarc felt there was no mission difficult or risky enough for Nereus, as if he was just waiting for Nereus to fail and fall out of favor. But after many successful operations, Nereus was more popular than ever.

One day, Ruarc accused Nereus of espionage, a charge that would've demoted Nereus to a lower rank and landed him in the brig. Documents indicated that the Ahti were plotting to overthrow Ruarc, but he lied and said that it was Nereus' doing and that he'd spied on Ruarc and sold his secrets. During the tribunal, it was one merman's word against the other's. When the truth prevailed, it was Ruarc who was disgraced and sent away, while Nereus took over the command.

This further emboldened Nereus, who had been accustomed to getting what he wanted all his life. His officers, including Dorian, noted that Nereus showed no emotion in victory or defeat. He simply persevered, keeping his feelings to himself.

Not only did he feel like he didn't belong anywhere, he trusted no one.

While doing reconnaissance around the Atlantis border one day, he felt a sharp tug on his tail and was soon pulled underwater. To his surprise, an Ahti merman had him in a formidable grip, but he quickly indicated that he had no intention of hurting Nereus.

"My name is Ea," the Ahti merman said. He had pale yellow eyes and icy green skin, with dark hair arranged in a single plait that traveled down his spine like the tail of a kite.

"What do you want?" Nereus said, squirming as Ea tightened his grip.

"We're cousins," Ea confided. "Your mother, Tethys, was my mother's sister."

"You know my mother?" Nereus asked, eyes wide. "Where is she?"

Startled by the sudden darting of a nurse shark, Ea looked around. "I want to make you an offer," he said. "I don't have much time. If you want to leave the Okeanos and join the Ahti, we will keep you safe."

"Safe from what?" Nereus asked. "And what about my mother?"

"They'll never let someone like you lead them," Ea said, loosening his grip on Nereus.

"Someone like me? But no one knows ..."

And then it dawned on him. Ruarc had traveled in the same circles as Phirun. Surely, that was the reason he'd made Nereus the target of his resentiment. Perhaps that's why Phirun spilled his angry secrets that night. The truth had come out.

A gam of tiger sharks began to swarm, and Ea let go of Nereus.

"I have to go," he said. "Don't forget. They will betray you. You would do well to use any asset and be prepared to negotiate if necessary, cousin."

"Wait, what about my mother?" Nereus called out. "Is she still alive?"

But it was too late. Ea was gone, his thick tail undulating through the water until it disappeared from Nereus' sight.

"Sir," Dorian said, pulling Nereus from his thoughts as he watched the crew of the *G2* preparing their stations. "What are your plans to battle the Ahti? The troops are, well, concerned."

Again with the doubt.

Nereus had been hearing it for months. They thought he hadn't done enough to protect Kairus. They'd lost confidence in him ever since that day that Avery had terrorized him. They wanted to retreat to Atlantis, where Nereus had vowed to never return. He knew his troops were loyal in name only. They spoke nothing but disrespect behind his back.

Just like that day when Avery had menaced him with his ship, Nereus was caught between two unfavorable scenarios. Stay and lead the Okeanos while his power slips away and risk being overthrown. Or offer his treasure to the Ahti as a gesture of good faith, in hopes that they will accept him. It was well known that the Ahti ruler, Ibai, was fond of luxury. The Eye of India would make a splendid offering and likely afford Nereus the life of comfort he'd long forgotten.

"Sir?" Dorian repeated. "What are your plans?"

"Well," Nereus began. "I suppose that depends on how cooperative our guests are going to be."

"It appears they've been working on strategy," Dorian said. "But we'll all need to work together."

Nereus glared at Dorian. He'd had enough of this subordinate telling him what to do.

"Is that so?"

"Sir, it's just my opinion, but—"

"You can keep your opinion to yourself, general," Nereus snapped. "I'm still running this operation."

Dorian's gills ruffled measuredly, but his eyes had narrowed to an icy stare. "Then I suggest you start running it, sir."

"Is that a threat?" Nereus said, pushing himself against Dorian's broad chest.

They were eye to eye now, but Dorian refused to back down, holding Nereus' stare. "I suppose one might interpret it that way."

Nereus' voice was calm and hushed as he pushed harder against Dorian. "You listen here, general. I am not about to be threatened by any lower-ranking underling who doesn't know when to hold his tongue."

The two of them remained in a faceoff, unflinching and unwilling to concede. As their troops began to take notice, a growing murmur took over the murky depths. But everything went quiet as a thunderous roar came from the portside, and once again the *G2* began to shake.

{ eleven }

Minty jumped when she felt the *G2* lurch. Though she didn't need to look, she turned toward the portside and confirmed her suspicions. A thick, dark tentacle had the *G2* in its grasp. But this time, it wasn't alone.

Outside the protective bubble, a collection of sea creatures appeared. Here were the Ahti, arranged in formation on the backs of tiger sharks, giant crabs, and menacing sting rays.

Minty blinked in disbelief.

I thought they rode kraken?

She hurried toward mid-deck. But before she could get there, another jolt knocked her down and she bounced hard, sprawling on the deck.

"Minty!" called Carter, extending his arm. "I see our friends have returned. You all right?"

"I'm fine. But what are we going to do? I don't even know how to fight them," Minty said, struggling to stand as the ship rocked back and forth.

"Snowy's been working on that," Carter said, hoisting her to her feet.

"But I thought we'd have more time," Minty said as they ran across the deck. "How do we even begin?"

Just then, a loud, rhythmic thumping began, echoing over the *G2*. One by one, the Ahti and their sea steeds were knocking on the protective bubble, creating a reverberation that spread over the ship.

"What are they doing?" Minty asked as they tripped and stumbled their way to the ship's wheel where she felt most in command. Snowy joined them, spinning in her shoes as the ship shook again.

"Just harassing us, for now," Snowy advised, grabbing the wheel to keep herself steady. "This is typical, according to Lyr. They don't always attack outright. They will often threaten and taunt the Okeanos, forcing them to make the first move."

"That can be a very effective strategy," Minty said, nearly shouting to be heard over the pounding.

"And it can also backfire," Carter said.

Minty cocked her brow. "Oh?"

"Yes, it gives us time to expose their weaknesses," he explained.

Minty nodded, realizing she hadn't thought about that.

"Where's Nereus?" Snowy asked.

"No idea," Minty shrugged. "But we can't wait. Snowy, what do you suggest?"

"Well," Snowy said, "one thing we have to do is—"

They all tumbled together as the *G2* shook again. The crew was screaming and the Okeanos soldiers were struggling to stay upright on their seahorses and squid as the Ahti threatened them outside the bubble. As they untangled, Minty's gaze rested on a terrifying sight—the open mouth of the kraken.

"Whatever it is, let's do it before that thing eats us!" she yelled as Carter lifted her up from the deck.

"Remember," Carter said, "the longer they toy with us, the longer we have to pinpoint their weaknesses."

"But how are we going to fight while we're in this bubble?" Minty asked.

"The Okeanos have a special technology," Snowy said. "They used it to help sink this ship. You see, it breaks up sea water and converts it—"

"Like an air generator?" Carter asked.

"Yes," Snowy said. "Actually—"

"No time for details," Minty urged. "What do we need to do right now to stay alive?"

She trembled as the *G2* continued to shake. She thought about Goldie and how scared she must be. Minty was determined to stay brave, but this kraken thing was making it difficult. Then a confident voice echoed over everyone.

"Form a barrier," Dorian yelled, commanding the mounted Okeanos. "Line up around the perimeter of the ship and stay at the ready!"

With that, Dorian looked at Minty.

"Man your posts," she ordered. "Draw your weapons and load the cannons!"

As the *G2* crew scrambled to their stations, Minty turned to Carter. "If they break through the barrier, at least we'll be positioned to fight, even if it means we drown."

"That's where the air generator comes in," Snowy said. "That's what I've been researching. We're not sunk yet."

Minty and Carter swung their heads around and looked at her, each letting out a groan.

"You just have to trust me," Snowy said. "It's going to work."

Minty looked at Carter, who gave her a reassuring nod.

"Carter, take the wheel for a minute," she said. Then she ran to the edge of the bubble so she could get closer to Dorian. The *G2* thumped and rocked. The kraken's gaping mouth pressed against the protective barrier, exposing its sharp fangs and a glimpse into its cavernous throat.

Minty shuddered at the idea of being swallowed by the terrifying sea creature, but she knew she had to be brave. "I guess we're all in," she said.

"Then you'll get your favor," Dorian said. "You have my word."

Minty gave him a wink and stumbled back to the ship's wheel, her boots clunking across the deck as she fell. The sharks, sting rays, and crabs carrying the Ahti swarmed closer. A hefty whale loomed in the distance, with a white-haired Ahti on its back. Minty braced herself for impact. With a loud gurgle, the kraken undulated.

"Look at that thing," Minty said. "You can practically see all the way into its stomach."

"I have an idea," Snowy said.

***

"Everyone! Put on your oxidators!" Snowy yelled, and the crew followed her orders. She didn't want to think about what might happen if the bubble was punctured, but at least this way they wouldn't all drown. Assuming they survived this attack.

A line of crew members bordered the ship's rail, swords drawn and prepared to engage in combat if the Ahti broke through. Snowy nodded to Clem, who was ready at the Kotter cannon. Then she ran down the stairs, hustling to the steam chamber to make sure the massive air pot was in place. Rogers gave her a nod as she got to the doorway and she quickly made her way back to the deck. Goldie was huddled near the main mast.

"Oh, no, little one," Snowy said, screeching to a halt. "You need to be below deck."

"I want to watch!" she pouted. "I don't want to be by myself!"

"Goldie," Snowy began. "This really isn't the time to—"

Goldie screamed at the sight of the Ahti army coming toward them.

"Don't make me go down there by myself!" the little girl cried. "I'm too scared!"

Snowy swooped Goldie into her arms and ran to a large box on the deck. It held the super sail, but they'd used it to store a surplus of the personal air vases that kept the oxidators working. She threw the lid open and stuffed Goldie inside, nestling her among the billowy sail and colorful pots.

"Hide in here, but keep that oxidator on," Snowy said. "Do not take it off."

She replaced the lid quickly, not quite lining it up square. As she ran back to the ship's wheel, Goldie peeked out, her eyes glancing side to side.

"Minty!" Snowy said as she reached the wheel. "We're ready to fire on your orders."

"Closing in!" called Carter from the crow's nest, a spyglass to his eye.

"Get your oxidator on!" Minty yelled to him.

He pulled it on and held the spyglass up, then shrugged, indicating that he couldn't see.

Minty shook her head as he pulled it off again.

"Can't think about that now," Snowy said. "He's smart. He'll be fine."

"Two hundred yards," he called out.

"Right," Minty agreed. "You're sure these cannonballs are going to fly?"

Snowy tried to smile. "Yes," she fibbed. "And Rogers has the air pot positioned in the steam chamber. When you need to move, we'll be ready."

"And you're certain the bubble won't break?" Minty asked, her voice shaky.

"Yes," Snowy fibbed again. She couldn't be sure, but she knew she had to show confidence so Minty wouldn't be afraid. She needed her best friend to steer this ship, even if it meant certain doom. After all they'd been through together, she didn't want Minty to be scared.

"One hundred fifty yards," Carter yelled.

Minty swallowed hard. "Alright," she said, standing tall. "Prepare for battle! Load the cannons!"

Snowy watched as Clem went through the process, adding a little gunpowder ahead of each cannonball, and a larger amount behind, just as she had shown him. She closed her eyes as he finished his critical task.

This had better work.

Snowy opened her eyes and gazed into the distance. A swarm of sea life barreled toward them. There were so many creatures, the light had begun to eclipse. Sharks and porpoises, crabs and sting rays, spiny lobsters and prickly sea urchins of enormous proportions, all carrying the burly Ahti who wielded their spears like a band of assassins.

"One hundred yards," Carter shouted. "What are your orders, Captain?"

Minty looked at Snowy, who nodded. Then Minty gripped the wheel.

"Two volleys straight into the middle!" Minty called out. "Fire!"

Without hesitation, Clem blasted two shots, each bursting through the bubble and hurtling toward the oncoming Ahti warriors. They scattered as the projectiles split them into two groups, slowing their momentum. To Snowy's great relief, the bubble sealed itself up, just as Lyr had said it would. She exhaled hard, erasing the quiver in her throat.

Meanwhile, Dorian led the Okeanos troops on the right flank, while Lyr led the Okeanos on the left, each of them holding their positions and ready to fight. The Ahti on the outer fringes began to attack the enlisted Okeanos, positioned on the borders. Sharks and squid tangled together, while tridents and spears clashed. The lower-ranked Okeanos were holding off the stronger Ahti, for now, but Snowy could see that there were many more on the way. And something very dark behind them, still moving forward.

"Engage the thrusters!" Minty yelled.

"Thrusters ready!" came Rogers' voice from below deck.

Snowy thought about Fiz, hoping that he had completed his experiment. But before she could complete the thought, a familiar voice, in distress, caught her attention. She turned to see Lyr, struggling to stay in his saddle as an Ahti warrior astride a giant crab choked him from behind. As the crab's claws pinched his sea horse, Lyr jabbed his elbow straight up into the Ahti's jaw. The Ahti's head popped back, forcing him to loosen his grip on Lyr's throat with each elbow thrust. They wrestled until Lyr's sea horse yelped in pain, seriously wounded.

Carter shinnied down the mast, dropping to the deck and running toward Lyr.

"Noah!" Minty yelled. "Your oxidator!"

He got to the edge of the bubble, just across from Lyr and the Ahti locked in their duel. He pulled his oxidator on just as a riderless tiger shark crashed against the bubble. With its strong jaws, it snapped at Carter, penetrating the bubble and sinking its razorlike teeth into his personal air vase. With a loud whoosh, a burst of air escaped, propelling Carter into the ocean on the other side before the bubble closed. He grabbed the shark's dorsal fin and hoisted himself onto its back, then pressed his thighs against the shark's gill slits while kicking and holding down its pectoral fins with his feet.

Snowy and Minty gasped, watching Carter ride the tiger shark behind enemy lines. Meanwhile, Lyr continued to struggle, his sea horse fading from its injuries. The Ahti raised his spear, poised to drive it into Lyr's chest. But before he could, Carter zoomed in on the tiger shark. With its tail thrashing, it knocked the Ahti off his crab. Carter caught the spear and thrust it into the Ahti's side. As the hulking warrior's blood spilled, a gam of sharks dumped their Ahti riders and began to circle. The wounded Ahti fell toward the sea floor, with several sharks diving after him. His screams shook the bubble as they tore him apart.

"Oh," Snowy said, turning her head away from the gruesome scene. Her stomach curdled but she knew she had to stay focused.

Carter helped Lyr onto the tiger shark. Lyr dragged his sea horse by its reins until he could hand it off to an Okeanos soldier. Then they pulled up next to the bubble.

"Swim down below the deck!" Snowy yelled. "Get Carter below the bubble so he can climb through the gun port and board the ship."

With a nod, Carter and Lyr swooped down. Minty ordered another two volleys and Clem delivered, scattering the Ahti again. Some, after seeing the sharks feast, abandoned the battle and retreated.

Snowy watched Dorian and his troops holding off the remaining Ahti. After so many of them had been dumped by their sharks or deserted, the Okeanos now outnumbered them. The battle raged on, with the Okeanos taking advantage of the Ahti's depleted troops. With Lyr and his soldiers reinforcing Dorian's line and surrounding the Ahti, they systematically eliminated the majority, tightening their circle as they fought.

"Wait," Snowy said, "where's Nereus?"

Minty shrugged.

But there was no time to think about him. Snowy shuddered as the dark shadow inched closer.

"Is that what I think it is?" Minty asked.

"Kraken," Snowy said.

Carter stumbled onto the deck from the stairs. His clothes soaked, he leaned against the mast and gasped for breath.

"Carter," Snowy called to him, her eyes on the looming shadow closing in. "Round up as many of those small vases as you can. They're packed in with the super sail. Goldie's in there, too. Get some of the crew and take those vases over to the edge of the bubble."

Minty turned to her and raised a brow.

"Be ready," Snowy said. "We're about to have a blast."

{ twelve }

Nereus looked over his shoulder as the Ahti retreated. Then he turned back to Ea, astride a whale, and offered him the chest.

"Here," he said, "I hope you will consider the Eye of India a suitable gift in exchange for accepting me into this tribe."

Ea unlocked the metal latch and pulled back the lid, exposing an enormous, gleaming blue pearl. Even in the depths of the murky sea, it glimmered like the sun on a peaceful lake.

"Cousin," he said, the pearl's glow illuminating his face, "it will be our honor to have you rejoin your true brethren, the Ahti. This offering will help us refortify our defenses, but I'm afraid we will need much more."

Nereus steadied his sea horse as a wave went through the water. "The Eye of India is the most precious possession of the Okeanos," he said. "I don't know what more I can offer you."

Ea looked at the kraken slowly moving in behind Nereus, its tentacles nearly within grasp of the submerged vessel.

"We'll be needing that ship," he said.

* * *

Dorian and Lyr had managed to capture the remaining few Ahti warriors, binding them with kelp stipes and tethering them to the spikes of a massive sea urchin.

"Bring it down, Fiz," Dorian called. With that, a team of sea turtles began towing the urchin and its captives to the floor of the castle, where they were to remain until the Ahti negotiated their release.

The Okeanos troops dispersed, some taking up guard over their prisoners, others tending to their wounds, and the rest retreating to a spot behind the ship, to take inventory and wait for further instructions.

Nereus knew what he had to do as he rode up to Dorian on his sea horse.

"Sir," Dorian said with surprise, "we thought you had been captured."

"They tried," Nereus lied without emotion, "but I got away."

"That's good news, sir," Lyr chimed in from the back of a tiger shark.

"Lyr," Nereus said, "how did you wind up on that? What happened to your sea horse?"

"Injured in battle, sir," Lyr explained. "One of the Landers saved me. First Mate Carter. We owe him, well, all of them, a great debt."

Well, maybe not yet.

"I see," Nereus said, watching the kraken as it made its final approach. "I suppose we should see what we can do."

Lyr spoke up, "Snowy said she had a plan figured out. I think we should just let her handle it."

Nereus shot him an icy glare. "Let her … *handle* it?"

"Yes," Dorian said, setting his jaw. "She's shown true leadership during this entire ordeal."

Nereus turned his glare to Dorian, who returned it with equal disdain. But before Nereus could respond, a thunderous roar erupted.

As the trio swam toward the ship, the *G2* suddenly blasted through the water, escaping the kraken's grasp as a stream of bubbles shot out from below the hull.

"She's using the steam thrusters!" Lyr said. "She figured it out!"

But the ship began to sputter. Caught in a bubble wake, it struggled to maneuver, and the kraken threatened it again. Waves undulated in sync with the kraken's movements. Just as it got its tentacle around the ship again, the *G2* blasted this way and that, shaking the kraken loose and stirring up the water. But the ship seemed to be losing momentum as it struggled to move through its own wake. Then the kraken managed to get two tentacles around the ship, then three, holding it tight as it pushed itself closer. Soon, it had four tentacles around the ship, and then it was five. The ship was motionless as the kraken gripped it, dwarfing it like a child's toy.

Nereus and the others fought the surging waves to stay upright as they moved close enough to observe from outside the bubble. He watched Carter and the crew members line up against the bubble and hoist the personal air vases the Okeanos had given them. With six of its tentacles now wrapped around the ship, the kraken slowly rocked it from side to side, as if toying with it. Then, ready to finish the task at hand, it opened its jaws, pulling the ship toward its gory mouth.

"Oh no," Lyr gasped.

Nereus turned and looked at him, failing to understand his empathy for a Lander. But the young merman seemed genuinely concerned for this girl, who was now about to be eaten alive, leaving her ship behind for Nereus to claim.

"NOW!" Nereus heard Snowy shout. Carter and the others began lobbing the air vases at the kraken. One by one, they went into the kraken's gaping mouth, filling it with air. Its mighty roar soon turned to a gurgle. An ominous rumbling echoed throughout the water as the captured ship tried desperately to escape the kraken's deadly grip and jagged fangs.

"What is that sound?" Lyr asked.

"Its stomach," Dorian replied.

Nereus advised them to take cover but it was too late.

The kraken let out a series of belches, each louder and deeper than the one before. The water surged so violently that they had difficulty hanging onto their mounts. Then in a dizzying blur, the kraken exploded, bursting into millions of tiny bits, which rained down to the ocean floor like a cloud of phosphorescent plankton.

A raucous cheer came from the ship and Nereus huffed and rolled his pale eyes.

Time to end this Lander celebration.

* * *

Nereus saw Snowy, Minty, and Carter hug each other. A small girl with dark hair ran up to them and Minty swooped her up, nuzzling noses. As the crew celebrated, one by one they clasped their hands together and gave thanks. Then they collapsed, clearly exhausted.

Odd. I'll never understand these Landers and their rituals.

Snowy looked up and ran toward Nereus, Dorian, and Lyr at the edge of the bubble.

"Snowy!" Lyr exclaimed, putting his webbed hand against the bubble. "You did it!"

As her hand met his, her words tumbled out like a surging stream after a hard rain. "*We* did it! Minty was amazing. She knew just when to activate those steam thrusters, which worked perfectly, thanks to Fiz and his amphora down in the steam chamber. I can't thank you enough for that. Oh, and did you see Carter and the crew throw the air pots into the kraken? That filled it with air until it couldn't hold anymore and then—"

"BOOM! That kraken was sent packin'," Lyr replied with a laugh. "Yes, I saw."

Dorian echoed, "We *all* saw. Great work, Snowy."

Minty had joined them, toting the small girl on her hip.

"That was some skillful sailing, Captain Minty," Lyr said.

"Indeed, it was," Dorian added.

Nereus felt his green blood begin to curdle. All this praise was going to make him sick. He gazed out toward the ocean, where the Ahti had retreated, knowing they'd soon be back. And this time, there would be no escape.

"Snowy," he said, his seahorse nudging against Lyr's tiger shark. Her hand slid down the bubble as Lyr was pushed aside. "I must congratulate you on a job well done."

"Thank you," she began. "We've upheld our end of the deal. And now, you owe us our freedom."

"And," Minty interjected, turning to Dorian, "I believe you owe us a favor."

Oh really?

He wondered what kind of negotiations his second-in-command had been conducting behind his back. But before Dorian could reply, Nereus said, "Permission to come aboard?"

Snowy, Minty, Lyr, and Dorian whipped around to look at Nereus.

"What?" they said in unison.

With that, Nereus lifted his trident and punctured the bubble.

"What are you doing?" Dorian yelled as the Landers pulled on their oxidators.

Snowy and Minty screamed, "Get your oxidators on!" and the crew did as they were told.

"Relax," Nereus said as he slipped inside the bubble, Dorian and Lyr following behind. "It'll close right back up."

And it did.

"Never mind, everyone," Snowy announced. "You can take them off." Again, the crew did as they were told and went back to resting after battling the kraken.

"But," Nereus added with a sinister smile as he advanced toward Snowy, "I'm afraid I have some bad news for you."

"What's that?" Snowy asked, her voice shaky.

"Someone here isn't who you think he is," Nereus replied, then he turned and looked at Lyr.

"What does that mean?" Lyr said, positioning himself between Nereus and Snowy.

"It means you betrayed us," Nereus said. "I saw you give something very valuable to the Ahti."

"What? I did no such thing," Lyr insisted.

"I'm going to have you brought up on charges," Nereus said. "You will be discharged and exiled for your betrayal."

"You can't do that!" Lyr said, pressing against Nereus.

"Watch me," said Nereus, pushing him out of the way. Then he turned to the Landers. "Have you heard of the Eye of India? It's a lovely blue pearl, extraordinary in size and iridescence. In fact, it's the most valuable treasure the Okeanos have. Well, *had*."

"Had?" Snowy asked.

"Yes," Nereus said, "*had*. Because young General Lyr here betrayed his tribe by giving it to the Ahti. That's how they knew to come here. He sent them a message and arranged to give it to them if they'd stop their attacks."

"What?" Lyr exclaimed. "I would never—"

"But you did," Nereus said with a cold grin. "I saw you."

"That's a lie!" yelled the little girl in Minty's arms.

"How dare you accuse me of such a thing," Nereus said, pushing toward the young girl and trying to intimidate her with his icy glare. Carter stepped toward Nereus. But the girl furrowed her brow and stared right back at him.

"I'm not lying," the little girl said. "You are! I watched from my spot in the box that holds the super sail. And I saw you take a treasure box and give it to the big merman out there. When he opened it, there was a glow in the water, and it lit up your faces. Inside the box was a big blue pearl. You gave it to him, and he took it. *You're* the one who betrayed the Okeanos."

"Are you going to believe this little brat?" Nereus huffed, trying to laugh it off.

"Yes," Minty said, "we are. And she's not a little brat. Her name is Goldie, and it just so happens that she's incapable of telling a lie."

Nereus looked at all of them, staring at him with angry eyes.

"Even you, Dorian?"

"I believe the girl," his first lieutenant said, only to be interrupted.

"Look!" Snowy screamed. "It's the Ahti! They've come back!"

Everyone but Nereus turned around as the crew scrambled back to their positions. He didn't need to look to know that his brethren had returned and were about to surround the ship.

"Our troops!" Dorian exclaimed. "They're all separated. We need to mobilize them!"

At last, Nereus spun around, delighted to see the Ahti closing in from every direction. It wouldn't be long now.

"No, we don't," he insisted.

"But sir," Lyr said.

Nereus drew back his trident, then rammed the shaft against Lyr's ribs, crumpling him to the deck. As Dorian rushed forward, Nereus spun the trident, landing against his head with a harsh whack. Dorian staggered, stumbling over Lyr who was still groaning and clutching his side. Over the screams of the Landers, Nereus took his trident and pierced the bubble. A trickle of seawater soon grew to a strong flood as the bubble disappeared completely. The ship's crew scrambled to get their oxidators on. But after using so many of the personal air pots to defeat the kraken, they were in short supply.

"Are you crazy?" Snowy screamed. "What are you doing?"

Nereus took the wheel, his lips twitching into a calm smile as the Ahti took their positions.

"I'm seizing this ship."

{ thirteen }

Minty gasped as a swarm of Ahti warriors surrounded the ship. Goldie squirmed in her arms, while Snowy attended to Lyr's and Dorian's wounds.

With no bubble to protect the G2, Minty knew that not only could the Ahti get close enough to engage in hand-to-hand combat, it would only be a matter of time before the crew ran out of air.

"Goldie, run down and hide in my quarters," Minty said, setting her down on the deck. "You'll be safe there."

"But I liked my hiding place in the sail storage locker," the child replied.

And that gave Minty an idea.

"No, go down below where you'll have more air. Now!" Minty instructed. Then she sprinted to the lockers below the main sail, flinging them open, with Carter right behind her. Some of the Ahti had already landed on the deck of the ship and were beginning to attack her crew. She found one of the larger air pots, too big for a personal oxidator, but small enough for her to lift.

"What are you doing?" Carter asked.

"I'm not sure," she said.

"HELP!" Clem called out from the starboard side.

They both turned and saw that an Ahti had Clem pinned against the rail, the mermen's burly hands around Clem's throat. Nereus laughed from the ship's wheel, apparently delighted that chaos was breaking loose all over the deck.

"Go!" Minty yelled. "Help Clem! I've got this."

Carter hesitated until Minty gave an assuring nod, then he took off.

I hope this works.

As the crew fought the Ahti, Minty lifted the air pot as high as she could, then smashed it onto the deck. The result was an emergency bubble, forming over most of the ship's deck. This air pocket allowed the crew members without oxidators to breathe, and it kept the remaining Ahti warriors outside.

She looked back to the starboard side. Carter had jumped on the Ahti's back. With his long arms, he was pulling the Ahti away from Clem's windpipe, but he kept slipping.

"Noah! Be careful!" she cried out.

As Clem gurgled and started to slump, Carter grabbed onto the Ahti's long braid, hoisting himself back up. Then he clenched his fist and punched the Ahti in the temple, stunning the merman enough to relax his grip. As Clem slipped out of the Ahti's clutches, Carter helped the old man to his feet. Then he wheeled around and socked the Ahti several times in the face, knocking him out.

"You alright?" Carter asked.

Clem nodded, breathless. "Yes," he managed. "Thank you."

Carter put his hand on the old man's shoulder. "Any time, friend."

Minty turned her attention back to Snowy, Lyr, and Dorian. Lyr was sitting up, still struggling to breathe, while Dorian was sprawled on his side. Snowy had torn the pocket off her apron and was holding it against Dorian's head to staunch the blue-green blood trickling from his temple.

"That was good thinking," Snowy said as Minty approached. "That air bubble is just what we needed."

"I took my best guess," Minty replied.

"The only problem is, I don't know how long it'll hold."

Minty hadn't thought about that. "I guess we'll find out," she said. "Are they going to be alright?"

Snowy shrugged. "I'm not sure," she said. "Lyr might have broken a rib. It's dangerous for him to move right now."

"Oh no," Minty said with a frown. "But we can't have him just sitting here, vulnerable to attack."

She glanced over her shoulder and saw Nereus at the wheel, running his pale green webbed hands over the instruments and fiddling with them.

Lyr swallowed, his breath laboring. "I'll be fine," he said between gasps. His gills fluttered. "Don't worry about me."

Minty looked back at Dorian. "What about him?"

Snowy shook her head. "I don't know," she said. "He's losing a lot of blood and he seems to be drifting out of consciousness. I can't do much but apply pressure and hope it stops bleeding."

Minty snapped her fingers. "I've got it!"

She turned back to the storage crate and pulled out part of the super sail. Then she grabbed her penknife from the pocket of her dress and started slicing off a section.

"Will this work?" she asked, offering a long strip of the sail to Snowy.

"Yes! More good thinking," she said as she started wrapping the sail around Dorian's blue face like a bandage. "Perfect."

"He ... one ..." Dorian muttered, his eyes flickering open and closed like the flame of a candle near an open window.

"Sh," Snowy said. "Don't try to talk."

"HE'S ..." Dorian said forcefully.

"He's what?" Minty asked. "Who is he?"

Dorian turned his eyes toward Nereus.

Minty looked over her shoulder and saw Nereus busily tinkering with the ship's wheel. If he figured out how to get this ship moving, they were going to be in even worse trouble.

"Nereus? Are you trying to say something about Nereus?"

Dorian closed his eyes, struggling to remain conscious.

"He's ... one ... of ..."

And then his eyes rolled back, and he collapsed against Snowy's lap, his blood staining the white apron of her dress. Minty watched his gills quiver in a slow, measured rhythm.

"He's still breathing," she observed.

"Right, but for how long?" Snowy wondered aloud.

Just then, Carter yelled from mid-deck. Two Ahti warriors had grabbed him and had his arms pinned back. Two others were taking turns punching him in the gut.

Minty's stomach churned with a feeling of helplessness. Everywhere she looked, the crew was fighting the Ahti. Swords and harpoons were flying as bodies hit the deck. Dorian and Lyr were injured. Nereus was at the wheel. And there were more Ahti waiting outside the bubble, which might burst at any minute, ready to finish them off.

She looked at Snowy. "What can I do?"

"Go down to the hold," Snowy said. "Check on Ari and Silky. I gave them that project you suggested. Make sure they're working as fast as they can. We're going to need all the help we can get."

***

Snowy held onto Dorian, whose chest heaved as they huddled behind some of the ship's storage crates. His eyes fluttered momentarily. Then as he let out a loud cough, they opened wide.

"Stay with me," Snowy said, nodding as he looked at her. "You'll be alright."

She could hear Nereus fiddling at the wheel and feared he might figure out how to get the ship moving, or worse, destroy the bubble protecting her crew. Then she saw Carter tying up two of the Ahti after disarming them.

"Carter!" Snowy called out. "See if you can keep Nereus busy while we move Dorian out of here!"

"On it!" he said, then took off running.

Meanwhile, Lyr had managed to roll himself closer to Dorian and Snowy.

"Dorian," Lyr said, patting the general's broad back. "Hang on. You're strong and you're the best fighter I've ever known. We need you now more than ever."

With a weak smile, Dorian mouthed, "Thank you."

"Clem!" Snowy called out, and the old sailor hurried over.

"Yes, Miss Snowy?"

"Clem, I need you to get Dorian somewhere safe," she explained. "He's in no shape to fight. Can you and Rogers get him down to the infirmary? You'll find Minty down there with Ari and Silky. They're working on something. Minty can help get him situated."

"You got it," Clem said. As he flagged down Rogers, a loud crack rang out. Everyone turned to look as Carter had landed a solid punch against Nereus' jaw. The Okeanos' leader reeled back against the wheel, dropping his trident, which Carter then kicked away. Nereus raised a webbed hand to his jaw and began pummeling Carter in the stomach.

"Go!" Carter yelled between blows.

As they dueled, Clem and Rogers gingerly lifted Dorian and hauled him below the deck.

Snowy then turned to Lyr. "Now," she said, "how are you feeling?"

He rubbed his webbed hand against his ribs. "Better, I think," he said. "But, still weak. I don't know that I'll be of much use. I'm sorry."

She watched his gills ruffle in a steady rhythm, proving that he was taking deeper breaths now. "Don't apologize," she said. "You've done a lot and need to rest. And besides, it's Fiz I need to help us right now, not you."

"Fiz?"

Carter rushed Nereus and dropped him on the deck. Nereus thrashed his tail upward, whacking Carter in the back. But as the first mate propelled forward, he straddled the merman's chest and delivered a series of elbows to the face. Nereus squirmed under Carter, grunting as he tried to wriggle his way free.

"This good?" Carter yelled to Snowy.

"Yes," Snowy said, "keep going! You're doing great!"

Nereus reached up and cold-cocked Carter against the ear.

"Thanks," Carter said, shaking it off before returning the punch to Nereus with double the impact. "Where's Minty?"

"Down in the infirmary," Snowy said. "Checking on Ari and Silky who are working on a special project."

"Is it what I think it is?" Carter asked, dodging another blow from Nereus.

"Something rather uplifting, yes," Snowy said.

Carter smiled and gripped Nereus around the shoulders and slammed him to the deck again.

"That's one strong lad," Lyr said.

"I know," Snowy agreed. "Getting back to Fiz, I have an idea and I'll need his expertise to figure out how to make it work, or if it will even work. It's complicated, but I feel like it could be the solution we need. How do I get him up here?"

Lyr looked around. Though the melee had started settling down and turning in the *G2* crew's favor, there was still a lot of fighting going on. "I don't know that we can. He'd be too vulnerable up here," he said. "But, there might be a way."

Snowy cocked her head. "Oh?"

"You see, Fiz has this very odd way of sensing things," Lyr said.

"Sensing things?"

"Thoughts," Lyr clarified. "I can't explain it, but I think it's how he comes up with many of his ideas."

"So, what do I do? Just think about my idea and he'll help me?"

"It couldn't hurt," Lyr said.

Snowy started to laugh, then stopped when she saw the sincerity in Lyr's pleading eyes. "Wait, are you serious?"

"Try it and find out," Lyr said, the color returning to his handsome blue-speckled face.

Snowy stared at him, but he just nodded.

"Well, here goes nothing," she said. Then she closed her eyes and concentrated on everything she'd been thinking about: eels and hydrogen and volcanoes. The images swirled together, and she couldn't make sense of anything. She waited, wondering what she was supposed to feel. When a sword bounced across the deck, she flinched. But Lyr pushed it back to a member of the *G2*'s crew and continued.

"Stay focused," he urged, his webbed hand covering hers. "Don't worry. I'll keep watch."

Snowy kept her eyes closed tight, distracted momentarily by Lyr's touch. But she knew how important this was. She concentrated on Fiz, trying to invoke him. Time seemed to be dragging on. But eventually she found that the longer she focused on her ideas, the less cloudy they became.

In her mind, Fiz appeared and explained everything, in clear, simple terms.

"First, I separate the sea water into four elements," he said, his weathered hands gesturing to a quartet of amphorae. "We have salt, chloride, oxygen, and hydrogen. Each element goes into its own vessel. The hydrogen we used to sink your ship comes from bubbles generated in a lava tube, part of an underwater volcano."

"And the volcano?" Snowy asked inside her mind. "How do you harness its energy?"

With a wave of his hand, Fiz made numbers and symbols appear. Snowy took in all the equations, studying them carefully, and suddenly her tentative theory made perfect sense.

"All we need is a conductor," Fiz said.

Snowy snapped her fingers and opened her eyes. "I've got it!"

"You figured it out?" Lyr asked, sitting tall now and breathing fine. He looked much more like himself.

"Yes," Snowy explained. "You were right! Fiz came to me and explained it all. See, he used hydrogen to sink this ship. And we're going to use it to take it back up to the surface, too."

Nereus swatted at Carter with his tail. Bruised and bloodied, they rolled perilously close to the trident, but Lyr managed to grab it.

"Traitor!" Nereus called to Lyr. "You know nothing of loyalty to your own kind!"

"Well, coming from you, that's rich," Lyr scoffed, stuffing the trident into the quiver behind his back. "Truly ... *rich* ... " Then he turned to Snowy.

"What?"

"That little girl," he said, "the one who saw Nereus with the Eye of India."

"Goldie?"

"Yes," Lyr said, his eyes focused on Nereus, who continued to struggle with Carter. "I need to ask her something."

***

Minty stepped into the infirmary. By the lamplight, Ari and Silky were nearly finished with their work among the vast swath of green fabric piled up on the floor and all around the room. The enormous silk balloon used to escape from the clutches of Kali and the toad men in the Caribbean was now fully repaired. Minty walked to the little table between the two bunks and looked at the plans Snowy had drawn up. On it was a diagram, detailing fasteners to be used to secure the balloon to the *G2's* sails. Minty studied the diagram and then looked back at what the spiders had done.

"You've been very busy," Minty said to the spiders.

"Miss Snowy told us it was urgent," Silky said as Ari continued to spin her threads.

"How much longer do you think it will take to finish?" Minty asked.

Silky shrugged, lifting six legs while standing on the other two. "I'm not sure," he said. "Probably not very long, but I know Ari's getting tired. She's been working nonstop and needs to rest."

A series of thuds echoed from above and Minty caught her breath, thinking about Noah and the others battling the Ahti.

"What's going on up there?" Silky asked.

Minty exhaled. "Our crew is fighting the Ahti, but don't you worry about that," she assured. "We'll all be fine. Snowy has a plan and I'm sure it's going to work."

"Fighting?" Silky said.

Just then, the infirmary door swung open. Clem backed into the room, cradling Dorian's head and nearly tripping on the green silk.

"We need space for him to recover," Clem announced. Then he motioned his head toward the infirmary bunks.

Minty rushed over to clear the fabric from one of the beds as Clem and Rogers gently laid Dorian down. The merman let out a soft groan but smiled when he saw Minty.

"How are you feeling?" she asked, carefully propping up his head as Clem and Rogers arranged his tail on the mattress.

Dorian spoke softly. "More upset than anything," he said. "I should've seen this coming."

"You can't blame yourself," Minty said, fluffing up the pillow. "How could you have known Nereus was going to betray everyone?"

"It was there all along," Dorian rasped.

Minty drew back. "What do you mean?"

Dorian hesitated, his gills laboring.

"He needs to rest," Clem said. "And we need to get back to the deck. Keep an eye on him."

"Sure," Minty said. "How's, uh, how's everyone doing up there?"

Rogers smiled from the doorway. "He's fine, Minty."

She wrinkled up her nose. *"He?"*

Clem pushed Rogers out the door and shook his head. "Everyone is fine," he said with a slight chuckle. "Don't worry. I'll look after ...

everyone. And I assure you, the *G2* is in good and capable hands. But we could use a captain as soon as you're done down here."

Minty nodded. "Thanks, Clem. I'll be up as soon as I can."

He winked as he closed the door.

"First Mate Carter is very strong and brave," Dorian observed, his voice growing stronger.

"Oh," Minty feigned surprise. "I'm concerned about all of my crew. This is a dangerous situation."

Dorian lifted a webbed hand and set it atop hers. "I've been around a long time," he said.

Minty squeezed his hand. "And I'm going to make sure you're around for a lot longer," she said.

"What I mean is that men like Carter are few and far between," he said, his breathing beginning to even. "You're lucky to have each other."

Minty felt herself blush. "Well," she said, clearing her throat unnecessarily, "tell me, how is it you can breathe down here? I thought you could only breathe air for a short while."

"That's a common misconception," Dorian said. "First of all, over generations, the Okeanos have developed the ability to breathe oxygen longer than other mermen tribes, such as the Ahti. And of course, my military training has only enhanced this ability. I suspect most of our more experienced warriors will be fine in this situation, at least for the short-term. Incidentally, we've also adapted to colder waters and near freezing temperatures."

"Wow," Minty said. "That's interesting. Now, what did you mean about Nereus? What was there all along, but you didn't see coming?"

"There has always been something different about Nereus," Dorian explained. "I noticed it when he first joined the military. At first I figured it was because he had a wealthy background."

"He did?"

"Oh, yes. His father, Phirun, was an aristocrat. Extremely wealthy, and wise, too. Very well-respected in our society. But he earned that respect by working hard to accumulate his wealth. It's no secret that Nereus appreciates fine things."

"Like what?"

Dorian took a deep breath, his chest rising. "Over the years, we've come across a lot of treasure," he said. "It's not uncommon. But for the Okeanos, gems and jewels have little meaning. We're not a society that thrives on material possessions. We all try to look out for each other. Yet, I don't think Nereus ever met a treasure he didn't like. He always got very excited about finding something left behind by pirates."

"Like Captain Avery," Minty mused aloud.

"Yes," Dorian confirmed. "Made a point of inspecting it all and, I suspect, keeping a few items that he just couldn't resist."

"Including the Eye of India?" Minty asked. Then she gasped, realizing she might have spoken out of turn, and dropped his hand. "Oh, I don't mean to get Lyr in trouble. Maybe I shouldn't have—"

"It's fine," Dorian said, patting her hand again. "That's a suspicion Lyr and I share. And it doesn't matter now."

"I suppose not," Minty said, relaxing her shoulders.

"But you're right," Dorian continued. "The Eye of India does seem to have special meaning to Nereus. I don't imagine that he'd ever give it up. So when your friend—"

"Goldie?"

"Yes, when Goldie said Nereus had given it to the Ahti, that didn't make sense," Dorian reasoned.

Minty thought for a minute, trying to put it all together. "Earlier, when I asked you to grant us a favor, you told me that you weren't sure you could trust him."

"That's true," Dorian said. "Because, in addition to his obsession with valuable trinkets, unlike his father, Nereus has always lacked the wisdom and respect that accompany a true leader."

"Interesting," Minty said. Then she sat up straight, remembering something. "Dorian, when we were up on the deck earlier, before you passed out, you were trying to tell us something."

"I was? I don't remember." He rubbed his head, clotted with green blood where he'd taken the blunt end of Nereus' trident.

"Yes, you said, 'He's one of …' and then you passed out," Minty said. "Were you talking about Nereus?"

More thuds came from above and she tensed her shoulders and held her breath.

"Don't worry," Dorian said. "From what I've seen, your crew is going to be fine. *All* of them."

Minty smiled. "Thank you. So, you don't remember what you wanted to tell us about Nereus?"

He thought for a moment, then shook his head. "I'm sorry," he said. "I don't think I can remember."

The noise from above grew louder and Minty stood up. "Well, I'm sorry to do this, but I need to get back up there."

"I understand," he said.

"I just need to check on a few things," Minty said, moving about the room. She put her hand over the pocket of her dress and felt her penknife. Then she went to a cupboard and pulled out a small chest.

"What's that?" Dorian asked. "Your own treasure?"

Minty stuffed a pair of gloves in her pocket, then unfastened the metal latch and lifted the lid. "Sort of," she said, spying the blue icicle as she peeked inside. Then she closed the chest again and tucked it under her arm.

As more thuds rang out, Minty looked toward the door.

"Go," Dorian said. "I'll be fine. You're a good captain, Minty. And your crew needs you more than I do right now."

"Be safe," she said, then she hurried out the door and up to the deck.

When she got there, she spied Snowy and Lyr, huddled near the mast. Several of the Ahti warriors had been defeated and tied up.

Clem, Rogers, and most of the crew were focused on the few remaining Ahti, and they seemed to have things under control. Her eyes scanned the deck until she spied Carter. He was tangled up with Nereus, near the ship's wheel. Both of them were breathing hard, but Carter smiled when he saw her.

Minty straightened her shoulders and returned his smile. Then Nereus reached back to elbow Carter in the ribs. Instead, Carter swerved and managed to grab Nereus by the wrists. In one swift move, Carter pinned Nereus' arms behind him, then drove his knee into the merman's back, dropping him onto the deck.

"Ready to surrender?" Carter asked.

Minty watched the erratic way his gills moved as Nereus gasped for breath, and she had a realization.

He's. One. Of—

While Carter bore down, Minty slowly walked toward the two of them, holding the icicle chest in front of her.

"Hi Noah," she said brightly, lifting the chest and nodding at him. "Everything all right?"

Just as she expected, Nereus' eyes followed her as she passed.

"Everything's just fine," shoving his knee deeper into Nereus' back. As the merman let out a hoarse groan, Carter added, "Your hair smells great today, by the way."

She giggled and kept walking until she reached Snowy and Lyr.

"And that's how we'll use the lava tube," Snowy was saying as Minty walked up. Then she looked at Minty. "How's the balloon?"

"Just about done," Minty reported.

"Good, we're going to need it soon, I think," Snowy said. Then she pointed to the icicle chest. "What are you doing with that?"

"Laying a trap," Minty said, putting on the gloves.

{ **fourteen** }

Nereus flopped onto the deck, feebly writhing to escape Carter's grip. His chest, scarred and bloodied, heaved. A low, wheezy gurgle escaped as he tried to steady himself. His half-Ahti lungs were spent; he never suspected he'd be stuck in this bubble for so long and he longed to get back into the sea where he could rely on his gills again. With all the might he had left, he drew up his tail and tried to sweep it against Carter's ankles. By now, beaten and broken, this seasoned warrior had little left in his arsenal. With the prospect of his imminent defeat setting in, he had reverted to the most basic techniques of combat.

Carter stumbled but managed to stay upright. "You ready to give up?" the young man asked.

Nereus gathered his withering strength and hurled a wad of spit against Carter's legs. "NEVER!"

"Your choice," Carter said, driving a boot into Nereus' rib cage. "I can do this all day."

Nereus looked around the deck, his vision blurry. All the Ahti had been beaten and tied up now, their braided heads hung with the shame of defeat. The *G2*'s crew members were divided between keeping watch on their captives and restoring order to their ship. He spied Lyr, smiling as he talked to Snowy. But Dorian was nowhere to be seen.

After all these years, my trident finally succeeded in hitting its mark. No matter what happens to me, at least that ungrateful toady won't ever have the satisfaction of being in charge.

Then he noticed Minty, and the small chest she'd carried past him earlier. Though weak and exhausted, he wondered what kind of treasure might wait inside. It must be something rare and precious to be stored in such a special manner.

His head grew heavy as his vision continued to blur. Nereus felt himself slipping away. His gills pulsed erratically, and he closed his eyes. Instantly, he was enraptured by a vision of his childhood home, bathed in dazzling white light. His father, Phirun, held a golden trident aloft as he demonstrated combat techniques. Behind him was a large portrait of Nereus' mother, Tethys. She had long dark hair, cool green eyes, and a wistful smile. Only knowing her through images, Nereus was still awed by her beauty and often wondered what kind of mother she would've been. Phirun rarely spoke of her. Nereus always assumed his father had avoided the topic because he was consumed with grief, until he learned the truth of her identity.

Over time, he memorized the portrait, gazing at it daily in the hopes of building a connection to her. He could picture her radiant face in his dreams, lending him comfort when he felt alone. He imagined the texture of her thick, dark hair, tumbling in waves along her shoulders. Resting on her collarbone was a necklace Phirun had given her, layered with exotic pearls of every color. At the center was an enormous blue pearl, the Eye of India.

Nereus focused on it in his mind and felt his waning strength surge through his body. Then he bolted up, taking Carter by surprise. With a vigorous shove, he knocked Carter back, slamming his head into the mast.

At once, Minty ran to him. "Noah!" she shouted, still clutching the little chest. She leaned over Carter, checking his wounds.

"You think we're defeated," Nereus sneered as he gripped the ship's wheel for balance. "We will never be defeated. I'll see to that."

Carter groaned. "What do you mean we?" he managed.

Nereus cackled. "You'll see," he said.

Minty stood up and stared at Nereus. "He means the Ahti," she said. "He's one of them."

A chorus of gasps spread across the ship's deck.

"Is that true?" Snowy asked.

There was no going back now. And nothing to lose.

"Yes," Nereus said with pride. "From my mother's side."

"Traitor!" Lyr shouted as he rushed forward.

His lungs aching, Nereus stood his ground. "I'm seizing this ship once and for all. And," he said, his eyes turning toward Minty, "I'll take whatever's in that box."

"You and what army?" Snowy said. "Look around, Nereus. This is over. Your men have been defeated."

Nereus laughed again. "No, you look around. Your crew is exhausted. Carter and Lyr are injured. And Dorian is gone."

Minty and Snowy exchanged a glance.

"Without them," Nereus continued, "it's just you girls against me. I'll have my brothers released and make quick work of you both. You can't stop me."

Snowy started to speak, but Minty interrupted.

"Wait," she said, backing up toward the ship's railing, holding the little chest at arm's length. "You want what's in this box? You want our treasure?"

Snowy quietly moved behind Nereus, who was following Minty.

"I can make you a deal," Minty pleaded, continuing toward the rail and the edge of the bubble.

His eyes fixed on the little chest with metal fittings, trying to imagine what must be inside. Coins? Or perhaps a collection of priceless gems. Either way, it would certainly help to establish his position in the Ahti society, and he'd never have to work again.

Minty fiddled with the lid as she leaned back against the rail.

"You want to see what's inside?" she teased.

Nereus nodded with greed, edging closer to her.

"If I give it to you, will you let us go?" Minty asked.

Nereus paused. "Let's see what it is first," he reasoned, unaware that Snowy had moved to within a step behind him.

"I told you," Minty explained. "It's our greatest treasure. Now, if I give it to you, will you let us go?"

Nereus knew the time for negotiations had long passed. They'd all be dead soon. But, he decided to play along.

"Of course," he lied. "Just give me that treasure and you'll all have your freedom. I promise."

***

Minty looked at Snowy, a step behind Nereus, and they exchanged a subtle wink. From what Lyr and Snowy had told her about the lava tube, she figured they were close to its center by now. She held the little icicle chest in front of her and watched Nereus follow it with his eyes.

"Oh, it's quite the treasure, indeed," Minty assured.

With heavy breaths, Nereus steadied himself. "What ... what kind of treasure?"

Minty watched him sag toward the deck then right himself again.

"Something I guarantee you've never seen before," Minty said. "In fact, it's so rare, that I can safely say it's the only one of its kind in the entire world."

Nereus twitched his lips into a reedy smile.

"And," Minty continued, "you promise that if we give this to you, that you'll let us all go?"

Nereus nodded slowly, his strength clearly fading as his breathing became more labored.

Minty looked him up and down and raised a brow. "What do you think, Snowy? Would you say he's earned this?"

"I don't know," Snowy said from over Nereus' slumping shoulder. "It seems that for a leader, Nereus hasn't treated his people very well. I mean, Lyr and Dorian did most of the work in the battle, and then Goldie saw him sell out the Okeanos and give away the Eye of India to one of the Ahti."

"Ea," Nereus stammered. "And he'll be returning soon. He's my cousin."

"Oh, just a big family reunion here, is it?" Minty asked, her gloved fingers rapping on the top of the chest as she backed up again.

"On my mother's side," Nereus repeated. "The Eye of India belonged to her. It was a gift from my father, and I gave it to Ea as a gesture of good faith, which he accepted to let me join the Ahti society."

"Is that why Dorian said you'd never give it up?" Minty asked.

Nereus scoffed and let out a weak chuckle. "Dorian," he said, breathing heavily. "Like he knew anything. I'm glad he's gone."

"Is that right?" Minty said, backing up again. With each step, Nereus haltingly slid himself against the ship's rail, leading him exactly where she wanted him to be.

"Yes," Nereus fumed, spittle forming on his lips. "He always worked against me. A second in command needs to be supportive, not questioning my motives. When you tossed him over the side, I'll bet he was barely decent chum for the sharks and eels that swim in this part of the ocean."

Minty opened her mouth, but Snowy interrupted.

"Did you say eels?" Snowy asked.

In the background, Minty could see that the green silk balloon had been brought up from the infirmary and that Silky and Ari were busy fastening it to the ship. Then she saw Clem helping Dorian. Soon, Carter and Lyr joined them, the crew members guiding the ailing mermen. Together, the four of them made their way toward an unsuspecting Nereus.

"Yes," Nereus said, holding onto the rail to keep his balance. "It used to be rare for them to come this far north, but there are plenty of them now. They particularly like to swarm in this area, just below a ship."

Minty saw Snowy's eyes widen and suspected she knew what Snowy might be thinking. "I had no idea," she said. "Did you know that, Snowy?"

"No," she said, leaning closer to Nereus. "And what about Fiz? You've not treated him very well, leaving him at the bottom of the ocean to fend for himself when the Ahti arrived."

"What do you know about Fiz?" Nereus sputtered, wheeling around to address Snowy.

"That he's very kind," Snowy said, holding Nereus' tottering gaze. "And brilliant. He taught me about the volcanoes on the sea floor and how he's trying to harness their energy."

"Yes," Nereus wheezed, "he's brilliant, no argument there. But he's too old and foolish to be of any use to us anymore."

"Well," Snowy said, "I'm not sure I'd say that just yet."

Minty took one more step back, and Nereus followed. Right where she wanted him. With Dorian and Lyr within earshot now, she danced her fingers over the chest's lid. It was time to give Nereus what he deserved. "So," she said, "should I let him have it?"

"Yes," Snowy with a deceptive smile. "I'd say he's earned it. Let him have it."

Minty slowly opened the chest's lid, feeling the chill of the blue icicle inside. With a gloved hand, she hovered over it, waiting. She raised her eyes to Snowy, who nodded, while Carter, Clem, Lyr, and Dorian looked on.

"Oh, let me have that!" Nereus yelled, lunging forward and snatching the chest out of Minty's hands. When he did, Snowy shoved Nereus toward Minty.

"You care more about treasure than your own people," Minty said, wielding the icicle.

Nereus tried to rush her but stopped when his eyes fell on Dorian. Stunned to see him alive, Nereus clutched the chest, then swatted Minty away as he struggled to feel around inside.

"It's empty!" he screamed, his back against the rail. "Now you'll never get your ship back!"

As Dorian, Lyr, Carter, and Clem came toward Nereus, Minty lunged, driving the icicle into his heart. Still holding the chest, he fell back, breaking through the bubble. Everyone put on their oxidators and crowded the rail to watch. Lyr and Dorian flicked their tails, free to swim again.

"Lyr!" Snowy yelled, "grab that hose from the hydrogen tank and bring it up here!"

"No!" Dorian said, placing his webbed hand on Lyr's chest. "I'll do it." Then he raced down to the volcano and carefully retrieved the hose. Minty could see that the steam-heated water was burning Dorian, but the strong merman general kept swimming, completing his mission.

"Get it to the balloon!" Snowy said, and Clem and Rogers took it from Dorian, who had collapsed on the deck, his scales scorched.

Frozen solid with the chest still in his hands, Nereus' face was permanently fixed in an expression of rage. He rested against the rail like a ghoulish statue. Lyr swam up to him and looked into Nereus' cold eyes.

"Goodbye, traitor," he said. Then he pushed Nereus over the edge. Rapidly, Nereus plummeted toward the volcano. Just as he reached the mouth of the lava tube, a group of large, dark eels swam by, foretelling Nereus' fate.

ZAP!

{ fifteen }

Snowy watched from inside her oxidator as Nereus' frozen body was surrounded by a swarm of eels. They tangled themselves around him, entwining their long dark bodies with smooth yellowish undersides. As the eels let out high-pitched screams, what looked like bolts of lightning encircled Nereus. With a spine-tingling crackle, Nereus was soon bathed in the blue-white sparks. Twitching and convulsing, he reached the lip of the volcano. Soon his hands spasmed, releasing the chest that had contained the icicle.

As Nereus descended into the volcano, the light continued to spark and pulse around him. Unknotted, the eels swam away. Snowy gasped. Soon the only screams she heard belonged to Nereus.

Fearing the special box that held one of the most powerful weapons in their arsenal might be lost, Snowy furrowed her brow. She knew she needed that box to contain the icicle safely. She was disappointed in herself for not thinking this through. But as her heart raced, her anxious thoughts suddenly turned.

Everything will be fine, she heard a voice say.

And as it did, Fiz emerged from his workshop, snagging the chest with a long-handled net fashioned from kelp. Before she could catch her breath, Fiz had secured the chest to one of his large sea turtles and sent it back up to the ship.

Snowy leaned over the railing as far as she could and waved to Fiz, silently expressing her gratitude. He replied by putting his warped, webbed hands together, as if in prayer, and nodding. Then he separated them and waved before retreating into his workshop.

Meanwhile, the sea turtle had reached the ship, and Carter quickly untethered the chest and handed it to Minty. Once she got the icicle back inside, she closed the lid and fastened the latch.

As she did, Clem waved his cap, indicating that Silky and Ari had finished fastening the balloon to the ship.

"Alright," Snowy said, "it looks like we're just about ready."

"Crew!" Minty yelled. "Man your posts! Get ready to set ... sail?"

As everyone scrambled about, the Okeanos clustered around Dorian, still in a heap on the edge of the deck. A few of the *G2*'s crew members grumbled about not being able to fulfill their duties.

"Give them room," Snowy urged. "Show some respect."

Dorian's breath came in slow bursts now. His scales singed, his tail warped. With a dull, fading gaze, he placed his hand on Lyr's shoulder.

"It's up to you now, general," he whispered. "Even if I survive this, I'll be in no shape to lead. That's your duty now."

"No!" Lyr cried, placing his hand over Dorian's. "You're the true leader of the Okeanos now. It should've been you all along. You've earned it far more than I ever could."

"What's done is done," Dorian sighed.

"What about this?" Goldie cried, pushing her way to the front of the group gathered around Dorian. In her hands was an extra oxidator. "Can't you use this?"

Dorian smiled at the little girl, his eyes regaining a bit of light. "Little one," he said, "that's very kind of you. But I'm afraid it won't work for me. Those are only for Landers. And besides, I'm afraid my injuries are too severe."

He groaned in pain and Lyr helped him into a more comfortable position.

"I want you to know," Lyr said, "that for as long as I have served, I have looked up to you. And I always will."

Dorian motioned for him to lean closer, then said, "Thank you, Lyr. You'll make a fine leader. But you must promise me one thing."

"Of course," Lyr said. "Anything."

Dorian looked toward Minty. "I told that young lady that we'd do her a favor someday," he said, his voice growing weak. "I need you to uphold that promise."

Carter put his arm around Minty and pulled her toward him. Then everyone watched as Dorian took his final breaths. Even the captured Ahti, still bound by their kelp ropes, bowed their heads as a sign of reverence for the veteran warrior.

With tears in her eyes, Snowy asked, "What do we do now?"

Lyr took Snowy's hand. "He always told me that death is part of battle," he said. "He wouldn't want us to be sad. But I'm afraid that sometimes it's a sacrifice that must be made."

"He saved all of us with his sacrifice," Snowy said, thinking about how Dorian had swum down to the volcano to retrieve the hose to the hydrogen tank. If it hadn't been for this brave act, they would've all perished. She stepped back and watched quietly with Minty and Carter as the Okeanos lifted his body and tied it to the back of the sea turtle, then sent it back down to its watery grave.

Snowy, Minty, and Carter joined hands and prayed for Dorian, and expressed their deep gratitude for what he had done. One by one, the Okeanos bid farewell and swam off, taking their Ahti prisoners with them.

"General," one of the Okeanos said, "we'll await your orders down at the castle."

Lyr nodded. "I'll be along soon," he said. Then he turned to Snowy. "I guess this is goodbye. But how is this going to work if you're still underwater? How will you get back to the surface?"

Snowy smiled, happy to have a chance to explain one last thing to this young merman who'd captured her attention. "It's very simple," she began. "You know that hose that Dorian brought up?"

She turned and gestured to the balloon, which was now being pumped full of hydrogen and beginning to inflate. "I didn't have much time to do the calculations," she explained, "but hydrogen is buoyant. Ari and Silky, our little spider friends, have repaired this balloon we used in the Caribbean and have spun enough silk webbing to attach it to the *G2*. Once we get enough hydrogen in there, we should be able to lift up out of the—"

With a sudden jerk, the ship began to rise. Snowy leaned against the rail, watching Lyr.

"Will I ever see you again?" he called.

Snowy shrugged. "Maybe when we need a favor?"

Lyr smiled and Snowy blew him a kiss as the *G2* began rocketing upward. As they zoomed through the water, Snowy thought about Dorian and how his kindness had kept them all alive.

With a splash, the *G2* burst through the water, and then it continued its ascent into the air, with the balloon and the super sail fully engaged. Snowy looked down and saw the islands down in the sea below. Everyone removed their oxidators and a loud cheer rang out across the deck as the crew celebrated their escape from the water. As they sailed into the air, the tropical breeze picked up, carrying them further along.

Some of the crew members began to cough and wheeze. The air was getting thin. Too thin. Suddenly, Snowy realized something was terribly wrong.

"That's too much hydrogen," she warned. "We're sailing way too high. Everyone get your oxidators on again!"

But before they could, some of the crew members began to collapse, falling hard onto the deck. Carter and Clem dashed to pull oxidators on everyone who had passed out, assuring that they'd be able to breathe while unconscious. Still climbing, the *G2* whizzed through the air. Then Snowy felt a strong force grab the ship and pull it northwest.

"What is it?" Minty cried, doing her best to stay upright.

"A gulfstream," Snowy supposed. "We're caught in it. There's too much hydrogen in the balloon and we can't stop it."

With a whoosh, the *G2* was sucked into the vortex, traveling at a high rate of speed to the northwest. With screams and yells, the crew began to panic. Minty furrowed her brow and then rifled through her pocket, pulling out her penknife.

"I've got it!" she said. Then she ran to the railing and looked upward, trying to figure out the best place to start climbing.

"Minty, no!" Carter yelled. "That's too dangerous!"

"It's our only chance," Minty said. "One of your books said that coming up from underwater too quickly would give everyone the bends."

"The what?" Snowy asked.

"You know, make them pass out," Minty shouted. Her jaw set, she reached up and grabbed part of the webbing Ari and Silky had made. Deftly, she swung her legs over to another section of webbing and then she climbed up as if scaling a cargo net.

"Just a small hole," Snowy called out, nervous that Minty would let too much air out at once and they'd drop as quickly as they rose.

"I got it," Minty said, working her way to the lower edge of the balloon. With her penknife, she pricked the tiniest hole. Then she crawled back along the webbing until she reached the mast. As she jumped down to the deck, Carter caught her in his arms.

"Great work, Minty!" Snowy called, but she was feeling woozy.

Sweaty and lightheaded, Snowy struggled to hang on to the wheel. She looked around. Although she could hear the small hole getting bigger and deflating the balloon at a steady rate, more and more of the crew were passing out. Queasy, Snowy tried to stay focused. Minty and Carter were collapsed together on the deck. Clem was cradling Goldie, hunkered down by the storage crates, oxidators on. One by one, the remaining crew members fell. As the balloon began to drift steadily, Snowy, too, passed out.

In and out of consciousness for hours, she wasn't aware that the *G2* had reached Bavaria. Drifting past a dark Bavarian forest, the *G2* continued on its path. Snowy was awake long enough to notice a large white oak tree, towering above all the others, as well as a stream.

Water. We can land in the water. We're saved!

"Minty!" she cried out, but no answer came.

Snowy looked around. Everyone was still asleep beneath their oxidators. The ship was already drifting past the stream, and Snowy was feeling woozy again. She looked down at the ground below, which was rapidly approaching. Her heavy eyes fixed on a farmer's field, lively with scurrying mice and chattering squirrels. It was the last thing she remembered seeing before she went back to sleep.

About the Author

Justin Mitson lives in Garden City, Idaho. A technologist and entrepreneur, he loves to write fun, engaging stories, from children's adventures and mob comedies to deep science fiction and time travel tales. Born in Butte, Montana, he spent most of his childhood roaming around the northwest, living in eighteen different locations before getting through high school. This gave him a sense of adventure and encouraged his imagination. A student of history as well as technology, Mr. Channing loves to ask, "what if?" When he's not writing, he's an avid water ski and snow ski enthusiast (and occasionally does those two activities on the same day) and loves to ride his electronic skateboard on the miles of the Boise area's greenbelt. Above all, his greatest joy is making his wife and two daughters laugh.

www.ingramcontent.com/pod-product-compliance
Lightning Source LLC
LaVergne TN
LVHW012024060526
838201LV00061B/4451